THE

QUARANTEENS

THE
QUARANTEENS

KEITH B. DARRELL

Amber Book
Company LLC

The QuaranTeens
Keith B. Darrell
Amber Book Company LLC
www.AmberBookCompany.com
U.S.A.

Library of Congress Control Number: 2020909131
The QuaranTeens / Keith B. Darrell

Address inquiries regarding foreign rights, translation rights, audio rights, film rights, television rights, or merchandising licensing to: *info@AmberBookCompany.com*.

First edition published 2020. Printed and bound in the United States of America.

All persons, places, and organizations in this book — except those clearly in the public domain — are fictitious, and any resemblance that may seem to exist to actual persons, places, or organizations living, dead, or defunct is purely coincidental. Stay home. Wear your mask.

14 13 12 11 10   9 8 7 6 5 4 3 2 1

ISBN 978-1-935971-54-2
First Edition • May 2020

This book is printed on acid-free paper. Your fingers are safe. E-book edition emits deadly radiation; you're screwed.

For **Amber,** who was there from the beginning and who will remain in spirit. And Banshee & Solo, too.

Intrepid proofreader Kayla Martinez perused this book for errors, but you know how hard it is to see clearly wearing a face mask. Beta listener Colt Taylor says he didn't see any errors but then he wasn't looking.

Special thanks to my characters, without whom I could not have written this book — for a writer is only as good as his characters; and to my readers, who inspire me and help me pay the light bill.

Legal Disclaimers: No characters were harmed in the production of this book. Actually, a few were killed off but it didn't hurt - they're all make-believe.

The QuaranTeens is also available electronically as a Kindle e-book and an EPUB formatted e-book. We're greedy that way. (Also available as a do-it-yourself audiobook — just speak aloud as you read).

Contents

Chapter One

—————————

THE MOROSE TEENAGER STARED AT the corpse. Rigor mortis had set in but the pungent odor of decay had not yet escaped its mortal confines. "I've never seen a dead body before."

"None of us has," her twin brother said glumly. "But we know what we have to do."

She pouted. "It's not fair! It'd be like killing him all over again."

Covid frowned. "He would have insisted on it. You know what the code says. He taught us what to do when this day came; when someone... died."

She gulped and nodded. "How will you get him to the furnace?" Corona asked.

"Best not to touch him. We can roll him onto a blanket. Four of us can pick it up by the corners and carry the blanket to the furnace. We'll have to burn the blanket, as well."

"Why? He wasn't infected."

"We can't be sure. He's dead, isn't he? Maybe it was a heart attack or his age but who knows for certain? We have to follow the code. The code will keep us safe."

Corona sighed. "The code will keep us safe." She repeated the mantra softly.

The four solemn teens hefted their human cargo through the vast underground concrete bunker. Dozens came out from their cramped quarters to watch the procession in silence borne as much from a lack of comprehension as from respect. Until now, death had been a stranger, the bogeyman of countless bedtime stories told by the one who had now succumbed to the dark threat from their nightmares.

The ersatz pallbearers bore the weight unsteadily. Ian was the strongest. The blond boy had the physique of a football player despite never having seen a football. His brawny hands held his end of the blanket slightly higher than the others as he trudged effortlessly ahead. The usually rebellious Kai was uncharacteristically silent. Corona had expected him to pronounce adherence to the code was no longer necessary, yet even he was subdued this day, solemnly obeying the code's most sacred admonition regarding disposal of the dead. Varian wasn't as quiet, though. The youth tussled his black hair from his eyes as he groaned. "He must have been eating twice our rations to be this heavy."

"Shut up, Varian," Covid said, as he struggled to hold up his end.

"You can't tell me what to do. You're not in charge." A smirk appeared on Varian's face. "Come to think of it, we'll need to choose someone to be in charge now that he's..." Even Varian couldn't bring himself to say the word.

2

Chapter One

Corona walked beside her brother. "There'll be time enough to discuss that later."

Blaine approached Kai. He was a slender redhead, slightly shorter than the other boys. "If you're getting tired, I can carry him."

Kai grinned. "I've got this, squirt."

Blaine fell back as the four boys carried the body ahead. "I just wanted to help," he said dejectedly. He felt a warm hand on his shoulder. Blaine turned and saw an alabaster girl whose auburn hair matched his own. "Fiona."

"I understand. That was thoughtful of you. But it looks heavy and the larger boys are best equipped to handle this."

Blaine nodded. "I just want to participate... to do my part; whatever that is."

Fiona hugged him. "You are. Simply by being here and sharing what we're all feeling."

"I've never felt like this before."

"It's called grief," Destine said. "I've read all about it. There are five stages: denial, anger, bargaining, depression, and acceptance. It was actually quite common before the quarantine—"

"Can it, Miss Know-it-all," Dax said. The freckled girl with the pixie hairstyle frowned. "He's hardly going to give you extra credit now."

"Just because you never cracked open a book or even set foot in the library is no reason to get snotty with me." Destine muttered, "Bitch."

The throng of 50 teenagers, ranging in age from 13-to-19, walked mostly in silence through the sprawling underground bunker, passing the bedrooms, the kitchen, the library, and the room where they had held classes. Destine wondered if the room would ever be used again now that their teacher was gone. He had been the last adult: the one who knew all the answers because he had actually lived outside the bunker before the quarantine; before they had even been born. He'd been able to fill in what the books didn't say and to solve any problems that arose. He'd said scientists like him were problem-solvers, although the teenagers only had a nebulous notion of what a scientist was. Some of the oldest teens vaguely remembered there had been a few other adults who died when they were very young. They were phantom memories and none could recall their names or faces. Presumably they, too, had ended up in the furnace. In those days, shortly after the quarantine began, they were most likely infected. But fire is the great cleanser. So the code said.

Covid, Ian, Kai, and Varian stopped at the iron furnace door. They set the body down and Ian opened the door. A powerful blast of heat assailed their faces and the bright flames lit up the room.

One of the younger girls timidly stepped forward. "Should we… should we say something first?" Nessa asked.

"That's dumb," Dax said. "It's not like he's going to hear anything you say. That's what being dead means."

Corona shot Dax a disapproving glance. Fiona walked over to Nessa. "I think that's a good idea, hun. You can say whatever you want."

A confused look appeared on Nessa's face. "I don't know what to say. It just doesn't seem right to dump him in the furnace like trash."

"It's the code," Varian said. "It's to keep us all safe."

"He's right," Covid said. "But, um, I'll say something. When we were born, or just a few years old, we were taken from our parents and brought here, to the bunker when the

4

virus broke out. None of us remember any of our parents, or even the other scientists who ran the bunker. He was the one who raised us. He cared for us when we were sick and taught us everything we know. We're all still alive because of him, and what he did for us every day of our lives." Covid turned to the body lying on the blanket. "Thank you."

A murmur of "Thank you"s spread through the crowd. "Anyone else got anything to say?" Varian asked. When no one replied, he knelt and grabbed one end of the blanket. "Give me a hand." Kai, Covid, and Ian lifted the blanket up and plopped the corpse into the fire. Kai tossed the blanket in after the body, briefly enshrouding it as both were consumed by vermillion flames.

And then, it was over. There was no fanfare; they didn't really know how to do death.

The teens scattered throughout the bunker. Most returned to the small, cramped quarters they called their rooms. Others went on with their daily tasks, finding solace in a return to normality. Coralie took the opportunity to lock herself away in her tiny quarters. She had always been a loner and preferred her solitude. She found interacting with the others socially awkward. She closed her door, knowing no one would disturb her or even bother to look for her.

Young Nessa wandered into the social area where a dozen older teens had congregated. She knew she wouldn't fit in with the more mature crowd but she was too frightened to return to her room alone. She saw Fiona and rushed to her, giving her an effusive hug. She crawled into Fiona's lap and rested her head against her chest as Fiona stroked her hair. She looked up at Fiona and asked, "What do we do now?"

"*That* is the question," Varian said.

"We do what we've always done," Covid said. "We've been trained our whole lives to survive. Nothing changes. We go on, as he would've wanted us to."

"Someone has to make the decisions," Varian said. "We can't function with fifty people making conflicting choices. We need a leader."

Kai sneered. "Let me guess: You think we should choose you."

"I'm the obvious choice. I'm one of the oldest. I have leadership qualities; it's documented in my file."

"How do you know what's in your file?" Corona asked

"I taught myself how to pick locks. They started files on us from the moment they brought us here. Psychological reports, genetic history… Apparently, I come from a line of strong leaders."

Destine grimaced. "If you'd spent more time in the library instead of rummaging through file cabinets you'd know before the quarantine people used to choose their leaders in elections."

"Or maybe it's time for a change," Corona said. "We've been stuck in this bunker our whole lives, or at least as long as some of us can remember. Aren't any of you curious what's on the other side of that door? There's a whole world waiting to be explored."

Covid's eyes widened. "You know we can't go outside. We don't dare. The code forbids it."

Kai grinned. "Rules are made to be broken. I think your sister's right. Or do you want to spend the rest of your life in this concrete hole?"

"There's a reason they built this bunker," Covid said. "When the virus came, it killed tens of thousands of people

6

every day. No one had any immunity to it. The old ones had never seen anything like it. They believed it would wipe out all humanity. All over the world, they rushed to build bunkers like this. Who knows how many actually succeeded? Certainly not many on this scale. Even so, we were limited to fifty small children and infants, genetically chosen to be the future of mankind. We have a duty to survive."

"We have a duty to live," Kai said. "I'm not going to stay here and bow down to Varian or you or anyone else."

"Don't be a reckless fool," Covid said. "What if the virus is still out there? If you catch it, there's no cure. What if the water and the plants and animals are contaminated? We have safe food and purified water here. The air is filtrated. And nothing out there can get inside."

"But that means we're trapped in here, as well," Corona said. "We may have lived here our whole lives but you've read the books; you know people weren't meant to live like this. You've seen the pictures of cities; streets filled with people; sunshine and sunsets."

"It's not like that anymore," Covid said. "Those books came from a time before the virus. We don't know what it looks like outside."

"That's the whole point. That's why we need to explore and find out. It's our world out there and we need to claim it."

Covid shot his sister an annoyed look. "Now's not the time for this discussion. We've suffered a great loss today. We should all reflect on that."

"Good idea," Destine said. "It's been a long day. I'll see you in the morning." She headed off to bed.

Dax frowned. "You may also wish to reflect on what'll happen when the generators finally give out and the lights go off; when we can no longer keep the furnace running; when the last of the food is gone; when we're cold and weak from hunger: Is waiting until then the best time to venture into the unknown — out of necessity?"

Covid sighed. "We'll discuss it with the others tomorrow. I want to hear what Destine has to say."

Dax frowned again. "What makes her opinion more valid than anyone else's?"

"Destine's the most knowledgeable person in the bunker," Covid said. "There isn't a book in the library she hasn't read twice. And she's smarter than anyone."

"Fine," Varian said. "We'll hold a group meeting tomorrow and hear her out. And while we're all gathered, we can hold an election." He smiled as he left the gathering.

Kai cocked his head. "He agreed too quickly. Varian's plotting something."

"Varian's always plotting something," Covid said.

"True," Kai said, "but this time there's no one to reign him in."

Covid grimaced. "We'll see about that."

The bunker had been hastily constructed by government military engineers and thus its design was utilitarian, not aesthetic. The initial scientists it housed realized the sprawling, concrete shelter would have to serve as home to 50 children so they did the best they could to disguise the cold, uninviting facility and turn it into a cozy environment with a homey atmosphere. Books in a room that became the library; curtains on windowless walls; a pair of saggy couches in what was to become the social area — these were the last-minute little touches that made a bunker a home.

Chapter One

But there was one spot they had missed; one oversight that put lie to the façade: the door leading to the outside world.

It wasn't an ordinary door. To the contrary, it was unlike any door one might have found in a home — or, at least, in a pre-quarantine home. It was metal… solid titanium, six inches thick. It was five feet tall, resembling a door to a bank vault or a submarine. The door was sealed with an unseen gasket, hidden inside its interior lip. There was a metal hand wheel on the door that had not been turned in a dozen years. For that reason, it was stuck and despite however much strength she exerted, Corona could not budge it.

She strained, both hands on the wheel, hoping to see it turn. So engaged was Corona in her efforts that she failed to see the figure come up behind her.

Chapter Two

KAI LEANED AGAINST THE WALL, cupping the back of his head in his palm. The others were asleep in their quarters and had been for several hours... except for the 16-year-old girl he was furtively observing as she quietly exerted herself attempting to turn the hand wheel. He stood in the shadows watching a while longer until he grew bored. "You'll never get it open," he said.

Corona jumped, startled by the voice coming from behind her. She pivoted. "What are you doing here?"

Kai shrugged. "Couldn't sleep. Can't wait to hear your excuse."

"I don't need an excuse to leave my quarters."

"Not to leave your quarters, but the bunker?"

"I wasn't—"

Kai's gaze fell on a sack propped beside the door. He grabbed it before Corona could object and looked inside. "Hmm... matches, water, food... and a knife from the kitchen. Sleepwalking your way through a scavenger hunt?"

Defeated, Corona drew a deep breath and exhaled. "You're right. I can't get it to turn. Are you going to wake everyone or wait until morning to tell them?" She felt Kai's penetrating gaze.

"Why?"

"I told you earlier why we should explore what lies on the other side of the door. I'm tired of living life vicariously through the pages of books written long before I was born. I want to touch and taste and smell all the things their words could never adequately describe. "

"But why now? Covid said we'd all discuss it tomorrow. Why sneak out in the middle of the night?"

"I know my twin better than anyone. You heard him: he thinks we should stay here. No change, carry on as before. Regardless of what Varian claims as his own strengths, Covid's the one who's a natural leader. Watch: he'll take charge tomorrow. Then, he'll order the door guarded day and night, or barricade it off so no one's tempted to see what's out there."

Kai nodded. "I assume you left him a note."

Corona shook her head. "Once Covid realized I wasn't in the bunker, he'd know where I'd gone. I guess that's a twin thing. We could always—"

"Read each other like a book?"

She sighed and her eyes drifted to the ceiling. "It doesn't matter now. I'll be spending my life in this concrete cage until the day they toss my body into the furnace."

Kai glanced inside the sack. "You don't have it."

"What?"

"Upper body strength. It's not your fault; you're a girl. You'd never have budged that wheel." He handed her the sack. "Put more water and food in there. Non-perishables, like crackers and tins." He reached in front of her and

12

grabbed the wheel, grunting as he turned it. "Hurry up; I'm working up an appetite."

She stared dumbfounded at him as the reality sank in. "You're helping me?"

"I'm coming with you; or at least leaving while I can. Now go get more provisions from the kitchen. Hurry, before someone hears us."

Esme lay in bed caressing Varian's arm. The sixteen-year-old girl looked longingly into his eyes. "Do you have to go now? Can't you stay a little longer?"

Varian sat up in bed and reached for his clothes. "You know better than anyone what a big day I have ahead of me. You did talk to all of them, didn't you?"

She slithered over to him and wrapped her arms around his torso. "I told you last night. I talked to everyone I thought could be swayed." She ran her hand along his body as Varian was dressing. "I can be very persuasive."

Varian moved her hand so he could button his shirt. "What did you have to promise them?"

Esme shrugged. "Hardly anything. I told Blaine he could be your assistant. He's such a pathetic, needy person," she said, with no trace of irony. "He wants to be part of the team, any team that will have him. He'll be eager to follow you because he doesn't want to be left out."

Varian nodded. "Will we have enough for the vote?"

Esme stared into his eyes again. "You know you can count on me. I'd do anything for you."

Varian smiled. "Yes, I know." He pulled up his boots and turned to leave Esme's quarters. As an afterthought, Varian returned to her and kissed her.

"I'll get dressed and meet you in the social area," she said as Varian headed out the door.

Destine arched her brow. "You look unusually agitated this morning," she said, joining Covid in the social area.

Covid frowned. "Corona wasn't in her room this morning. Her bed hadn't been slept in. I spent the last couple of hours searching the entire bunker. She's not here."

"That's impossible. You were just looking in the wrong places. There's nowhere else she could be."

Covid glanced across the bunker at the imposing metal door. "There's only one place I haven't looked."

Destine followed his glance. She frowned. "That's absurd. Corona would never go outside. It's against the code. If there are people left out there, they're probably asymptomatic carriers or infected themselves. She'd have to have a death wish."

"Or a wanderlust. I should have seen this coming. We'll have to go after her."

Destine cocked her head. "Madness must run in your genes. No one else must violate the code. We shouldn't even let her back in."

Covid looked at her in shock. "What are you talking about?"

"Corona will be breathing unfiltered air and coming into contact with potentially contaminated surfaces if not other people. This is a sterile environment. She could expose us all to the virus."

"You're talking about my sister."

"I'm talking about our lives. She should have known the risks... And the consequences."

14

Covid shook his head. "We have to look out for each other now more than ever. If she shows any sign of infection then obviously we can't let her back into the bunker but there may not even be any traces of the virus left. It's been twelve years."

"You're probably right. Of course, we don't know what's happened while we've been inside. The pandemic may have spread to every human on the planet. Worst case scenario, it may have killed them all. Or on the bright side, there may be survivors with antibodies making them immune. But your sister doesn't have any immunity and neither do we."

Covid grimaced and turned away.

"You know it's the only logical thing to do."

"She's my sister; relationships aren't based on logic. You'd realize that if you spent more time with people than books."

"You're torn, aren't you? I can see it on your face. You're tempted to go after her despite knowing how much you're needed here and that doing so goes against the very core of the code. Which will it be, Covid? Will you pursue the stray sheep or remain and tend to your flock?"

"You read too many books, Destine. We're people, not sheep."

"Some might argue otherwise. Varian sent his little lovesick butterfly flittering about last night to drum up support for his bid to lead us."

"What's a butterfly?"

Destine sighed. "Something that exists in books." She glanced at the door. "Or maybe out there. Never mind. The death of the last adult has created a power vacuum and Varian means to fill it."

"You realize I don't understand half of what you say."

15

"Then, maybe you should have spent more time in the library. I've used my time to learn as much as I can about every subject we have books on — science, history, politics, medicine — and I'm telling you, Varian is making a classic power play. This sort of thing has happened throughout history. Why, back in the Roman empire —"

"I don't have time for a history lesson. Corona is missing and every minute takes her farther away."

Dozens of teenagers crowded into the social area. Fiona accompanied Nessa, holding the young girl's hand reassuringly. The brawny Ian stood against the wall to make room for the smaller children. Dax ambled over to Covid and Destine. As more teens wandered in, Coralie stepped from her room following the crowd while not becoming part of it.

"Why so glum?" Tristan asked Dax. He wore a perpetual grin that looked as if it had been painted on his face.

"It's not normal to be cheerful when someone's died and the world's rapidly changing all around you."

Tristan gave a wide smile. "We're young and we're alive. How many others in the entire world can say that? There's no reason to mope about. You should seize the moment and enjoy every second of life. If you spend all your time worrying about what might happen you'll miss what *is* happening around you."

Dax sneered at the boy. "Sorry, I haven't had my happy juice this morning and I don't feel like taking philosophy lessons from a fourteen year old."

Tristan shrugged indifferently. He looked up and saw Varian and Esme enter, followed by Blaine.

Varian gazed out at the prepubescent faces, some as young as thirteen years old, and the countenances of the more mature adolescents, some like himself entering adulthood. "I see everyone got the message to meet this morning."

"Why did you call this meeting, Varian?" Keiana asked. She was a beautiful young woman, nineteen like Varian, but as knowledgeable as Destine. She shared Destine's thirst for knowledge and Varian's hunger for power.

"Yesterday was a painful day for all of us," Varian said. "Now that we're on our own, difficult days lay ahead. Our survival depends on what we do next. We must choose a leader."

Keiana smiled. "Very well; I accept the position."

Varian laughed uncomfortably. "I meant, we must choose the right leader. Someone capable of making the difficult decisions, the tough calls. As smart as you are, intelligence isn't enough. You're bright, you're beautiful, and you're well-liked; but this election isn't a popularity contest. It's about choosing the person who can keep every one of us alive."

Esme leaned into Varian. "You know he's right. When there are hard choices to make do you want someone making them based on how it affects her popularity? Or do you want someone more interested in making the best decisions even if you don't like him? The most important thing now is survival."

Blaine stepped forward. "I agree. Varian will keep us safe. We'll all have a part to play but Varian's the only one who can lead us when a crisis arises."

"Nice speech, Blaine," Keiana said. "What did Varian promise you in return for it?"

"We already have a crisis," Covid said. "Corona's missing. I think she's gone outside the bunker."

Corbin, a fifteen-year-old, looked around the crowded social area as he pondered how he might turn the situation to his advantage. This was the point where he expected someone besides Keiana to challenge Varian. If not Covid, who seemed preoccupied with his sister's disappearance, then the rebellious Kai who could always be counted on to object to rules and those who made them. Yet, he noticed, Kai was nowhere to be seen. "She's not the only one who seems to be missing. Has anyone seen Kai?"

Heads turned as four dozen pairs of eyes scanned the social area. "Two missing people," Keiana said. "It appears you have your first crisis, assuming you're elected leader."

"Varian's no leader," Covid said. "We can choose one later. Right now, we need to find Corona... And Kai."

"It'll only take a few minutes to vote," Varian said. "After all, the welfare of our entire community is more important than any single individual. Esme will pass out a slip of paper to everyone. Write the name of your chosen leader and place it in the box Blaine's holding." Esme stepped forward and handed out pencils and paper.

Covid grimaced but said nothing. After a few moments of reflection, the papers were scribbled on and placed inside the box. When the last teen had voted, Esme nervously took the box from Blaine. She knew how important the outcome was to Varian and she hoped her efforts the previous evening had paid off. She separated the papers and piles, plucking out one sheet. "One vote for Fiona." She glanced at thirteen-year-old Nessa. "How sweet!" She crumpled the paper and tossed it to the floor. "Fifteen votes for Keiana," she said, placing one pile aside and starting on the second. "Fifteen votes for Covid." Esme picked up the next pile and counted. "The rest are all marked for Varian

— all seventeen of them." She beamed at Varian, gesturing toward him. "Our new leader, Varian."

"Fine," Covid said impatiently. "Now what are we going to do about Corona and Kai?"

Varian mused. "They violated the code. If they were here, they'd have to be punished but they're not here. So there's nothing we can do."

"You call that leadership?" Covid asked angrily. "We can look for them."

"And violate the code ourselves?" Varian asked. "Expose all of us to the virus?"

Covid sighed. "A search party, then. Six volunteers."

"So had you been elected leader, you'd have us violate the sacred code and expose an eighth of our population to potential infection, all to save a troublemaker and your sister? I promised to keep us safe; I won't send anyone outside the bunker."

"He's right," Blaine said. "If it were anyone besides your sister, you'd be saying the same thing."

"How long do you think they can survive out there?" Varian asked Covid. "Who knows what conditions are like outside the bunker? If they're not already dead, they soon will be."

Covid grew angrier. "My sister's a survivor."

Varian smiled. "Then, you have nothing to worry about."

Covid clenched his fist. "I'm going to find them. Don't try to stop me."

Varian suppressed a grin at the thought of his rival banishing himself from the compound. "I wouldn't think of it."

"Covid!" Destine called out. "None of us has ever been outside but from everything I've read it's bigger than anything you can imagine. You may not be able to find them."

"I have to try."

"Let me grab my bag. I'm going with you."

Covid arched an eyebrow but didn't object. Likewise, Varian was too surprised by Destine's outburst to object either. A few minutes later, Ian tightened the hand wheel on the door after closing it behind them. Esme embraced Varian as a contented grin filled his face. The other teens chattered amongst themselves while Keiana contemplated what was to come.

Chapter Three

I T WAS DARK. DARKER THAN anything either Corona or Kai had ever seen. The only light visible came from a large, white object hovering in the sky set against a black backdrop punctuated by tiny flashing yellow specks. Corona looked up at it. "I think that's called the moon."

Kai stared at it. "What does it do?"

"Don't you remember when we studied astronomy? It's like a planet but not exactly. It comes out at night. It's really far away."

"Then, those speckling dots must be stars." He cocked his head and squinted. "I always thought they'd be bigger."

Corona dug into her sack and took out her flashlight. "I don't know how long the batteries will last."

"I'm surprised they work at all. They must be older than us. But I guess the scientists knew the best way to store them. Still, sooner or later they'll stop working."

"We won't need it when the sun comes out in the morning. I wonder what that will look like."

"I remember learning it was a star." Kai glanced up at the twinkling stars. "It had better be bigger than any of those up there or we won't be able to see much."

Corona adjusted her facemask. "Do you think these will protect us?"

Kai shrugged. "We'll find out." He glanced at the ground. "Shine the light over here." He kicked the illuminated spot of sand amidst the grass. "Look at it scatter. This sand stuff is fun. In the pictures it was always clumped together. That green stuff must be grass."

"Don't touch it," Corona said. "It might be contaminated."

Kai nodded. "Let's pick a direction and start walking."

Corona glanced back for one last look at the outside hatch leading to the bunker. Then, she hefted her sack over her shoulder and followed Kai.

Dawn was breaking. "It's getting lighter," Corona said. "We should see our first sunrise soon."

"I hope so. Maybe we should stop and rest." Kai sat down and took off his shoes. "My feet are killing me; I've never walked this far before."

Corona joined him. "No one has. We've been walking for hours. I doubt we'll be able to still see the bunker once the sun rises."

"It's so quiet. I thought there were supposed to be animals roaming about. The books are filled with pictures of all different kinds: lions, tigers, elephants."

"Maybe somewhere else. It's a big planet; we've only walked a little ways considering how large it is."

"My feet might disagree." Kai mused. "Suppose... Suppose there are no animals... Or other people left?"

22

Chapter Three

Corona chuckled. "If you're suggesting we become the next Adam and Eve and repopulate the world, then you're out of luck. Even if you turn out to be the last man on Earth, I'm not sleeping with you."

Kai shook his head. "That's not what I meant. I've never heard… Silence before. You know how voices carry in the bunker. Even the generators have a soft hum. There's always some sound in the background, even if you're not conscious of it. You never feel alone when there are dozens of people nearby, chattering away. But look out there: nothing. Sand and grass and nothing but the sound of our own footsteps."

"I can see the sun rising. It's as beautiful as all the books said it was. The pictures didn't do it justice. It's like a huge orange ball of fire slowly rising in the sky. I can't wait to see all of it."

Kai stood. "All right, let's keep walking. Now that we can see where we're going, maybe we'll stumble across someone else — if there are other people out here." Corona nodded and the two explorers set forth.

The oppressive sun approached high noon. Kai wiped the perspiration from his brow. It did little good as it was almost immediately replaced by more. "I've never sweated like this before; not even when I was exercising."

"The bunker is climate controlled. It's different outside."

"But why is it so hot?"

Corona gazed upward. "That's why. It's so bright I can't even look at it. It's awful. My clothes are drenched with sweat."

"Mine too. Do you think every day outside is like this? No wonder people built bunkers underground."

"Remember those trees we passed a few hours ago? We need to find more trees, or something we can hide under to shelter us from the sun's heat."

Kai pointed. "Over there. Way in the distance. I see something."

Corona scanned the horizon. "I don't see it. Is it a tree?"

Kai shook his head. "It's bigger than a tree if I can see it this far away. Not the same color, either. Maybe it's a building... Or even a city. According to the books in the library, there were lots of cities all over the world."

Corona pulled her canteen out of her sack and took a swig of water. "I hope whatever it is, we can find water there." She swished the water in her canteen, listening to it reverberate against the metal. "There's not much left."

"It's the heat. It's making us thirstier than normal. If we run out of water..." Kai left his thought unspoken. "It'll take us a couple hours to reach whatever that is. We could wait until dark when it's cool but then we wouldn't be able to see where we're going. Your flashlight can't shine on anything so far away." He looked at the younger girl. "Or, we could try to make our way back to the bunker."

"Remember those stars we saw last night? Our ancestors built spaceships and launched them into space. They didn't know what to expect or what they'd find. Some died in the attempt. But they did it anyway. Despite the risks and dangers of plunging into the unknown, they did. Ancient sailors did the same thing. It's what explorers do."

"Is that what we are? Explorers?"

Corona shrugged. "I don't know about you, but the books are filled with tales of men and women who ask 'What's out there?' and have to find out. I'm not turning back until I know."

"I just want to find a place where I can make my own rules and not live under someone else's. Life in the bunker may have been easier but I want to make my own choices; do things my own way."

Corona nodded. "Then, let's go on while we can still see whatever that is ahead." She offered Kai the canteen. He shook his head, deciding she needed the water more. Corona replaced the canteen into her sack. "And let's hope it has water."

A pebble that had slipped into Corona's shoe rubbed uncomfortably against the sole of her foot. She ignored the discomfort, not wanting to slow down to remove it. The small object on the horizon they had been heading toward had grown immense as they neared it, while the sun had begun to set, taking the daylight with it. Kai had wrapped his arm around her, the two supporting each other in their weakened states, dehydrated and suffering heatstroke. Kai stumbled and fell to the ground. Corona tugged at him. "Come on, we have to keep going."

Kai shook his head, beads of sweat flying off his face. "Let me lie down. I need to rest. You go ahead and I'll catch up."

Corona became resolute. "No, if we split up it'll be impossible to find each other again, especially once it becomes dark." She slid her arm beneath his underarm and helped him to his feet. "Lean on me."

"You're not strong enough to carry me."

"No, but I can support your weight. Just put one foot in front of the other."

Kai rose unsteadily, placing his arm around Corona's shoulder.

"Upper body strength my ass," Corona said. "I've still got one thing you don't."

"What's that?"

"Stamina. Now shut up and walk." They continued their grueling journey, shuffling forward toward a series of white buildings encased within a huge transparent dome.

Kai faded in and out of consciousness. Corona lugged the dead weight as she trudged forward. "Stay with me, Kai. Don't die on me." She wondered what life would be like if she survived, alone. Corona didn't want to think about it, but she couldn't help it. It was becoming a distinct possibility; assuming she didn't also succumb to heatstroke. "Well, maybe if you were the last man on Earth... And I was feeling desperate." She couldn't tell if Kai had heard her but she thought she detected a smile on his lips.

An hour passed. And then another. The sun had set below the horizon leaving only a soft glow to light the sky. The temperature had cooled but Kai had not recovered and Corona's head was pounding, her heart racing. With each step she forced herself forward. The canteen had been empty for an hour now. Sweat oozed from her pores, less from the sun's rays than from the fever now rising within her body as the heatstroke took its toll. She took one more faltering step and dropped to her knees. Kai slid from her weakened grasp and lay unmoving on the ground, either unable or unwilling to get up. Corona plopped face-first into the grass, her facemask plunging into the soil. Feverish thoughts filled her mind. *I should have said goodbye to Covid. But if I had, he'd have stopped me from leaving. Then again, maybe that would have been best. I guess he was right, after all.* She was too weak to lift her head, yet she noticed the growing darkness encroaching as twilight was slowly subsumed by the night. *It can't end like this,* Corona thought, her eyes shutting.

Twilight had not yet settled into dusk so the two bodies lying in the open were still visible. The evening was still and quiet. The silence was only broken by the occasional high-pitched howl of a hyena miles away but the two unconscious teenagers were beyond hearing.

A noise grew louder as a motorized vehicle approached. The modified Humvee stopped several feet from where Corona and Kai lay. From its mounted gun turret, a man swiveled his rifle as he nervously scanned the surroundings. The driver cut the engine and hopped out, cautiously walking to the still forms. He reached down to check their pulses.

"Are they dead?" the gunner shouted down.

"Not yet. But I've never seen anyone this pale before. Even with sunburn, they're white as ghosts."

"Hurry up and toss them in back before more Raiders show up."

The driver lugged each of the unconscious bodies into the back of the Humvee. "I don't think these are Raiders."

"What else could they be?"

"Dunno. Maybe survivors from some encampment or city?"

"Unlikely," the gunner said. "Unless their horses ran off; they appear to have been walking. They couldn't have walked that far."

"Maybe they had a vehicle. They might have been forced to abandon it if it broke down."

"Or they could have been dropped off by their friends in a vehicle. There may be others. We should resume the patrol."

The QuaranTeens

The driver shut the back door of the Humvee and climbed into the seat. "Not enough juice in the battery. If we don't head back and recharge it we'll be stuck out here." The driver glanced at Kai's unconscious form. "Besides, he looks young and virile. If he survives, we can count this as a successful outing."

The gunner grinned. "And if not, a couple of dead Raiders is still worth celebrating."

The driver chuckled and started the engine. The Humvee turned around and headed toward the domed structure, kicking up dust in its path.

Chapter Four

COVID WINCED AT THE SOUND of the thick titanium door locking behind them. Leaving the bunker had been the most momentous decision of his life and one he would rather not have had to make. Corona had left him no choice. He turned to Destine. "Why did you come with me?"

"You know as well as I do that Varian will make a shambles of things. When the others figure out they've made a mistake choosing him they'll need a true leader to whom to turn. That will be you: but only if you return alive."

"Meaning?"

"Meaning you won't last a day out here on your own."

Covid frowned. "I can take care of myself."

"Really? Have you studied biology? Can you tell which fruits are edible and which are poisonous? Have you read any books on medicine? Do you know how to clean a wound or set a broken bone?"

"Well, no but —"

"What about trailblazing? Sociology? Psychology?"

"Why would I need to know those things?"

"If we do run into other people and communities, knowledge of sociology and psychology will help us understand them. What about architecture? Can you tell the difference between a church and a school?"

Covid became defensive. "There was no reason to study any of that stuff in the bunker. It wasn't relevant; it had nothing to do with our lives."

"It does now," Destine said. "Fortunately for you, I *have* studied all those subjects. I can teach you some of what I know and keep you alive."

Covid grimaced.

"You're welcome."

Covid looked around their surroundings. In every direction he could see clear to the horizon. He had never imagined such vastness. "It's huge out here. How far does it go on?"

"A long, long way. I told you it would be nearly impossible to find Corona and Kai. They could've gone off in any direction. And we don't know what's out there: wild animals; contaminated environments; hostile humans. We don't even know if there's an uncontaminated source of food and water. Their odds of survival are slim... Just like ours."

Covid gritted his teeth. "We'll survive. All of us. Now which way should we go?"

Destine perused the ground. "Footprints. They lead that way." She pointed. Covid nodded and followed her. They walked for several miles before coming to a halt.

"What's wrong?" Covid asked. "Why have you stopped?"

Destine pointed to the ground. "The terrain has turned rocky. Boots and shoes don't make impressions on hard rocks as they do on soil. There's no more trail to follow. They could have gone anywhere from here."

"We should head in the direction we've been traveling in."

"That may work for a while. They probably continued in the same direction but at some point they would have veered left or right. There's no road or path for them to have stayed on. Even if they thought they were walking in a straight line they would have strayed in the dark."

"What do we do now?"

Destine shrugged. "We could go back the way we came and return to the bunker..." She saw the determined look in his eyes. "Or, we can pick a direction and start walking."

Covid wiped the sweat from his brow. "All right. That way." There was no logic to his choice, nor could there have been. All Covid knew was the one direction he couldn't choose was the one from which they had come. He was determined not to return to the bunker until he had searched everywhere for Corona. He just hadn't realized how massive "everywhere" might be.

Destine slipped off her facemask and sipped water from one of the canteens she had brought. She offered it to Covid, who shook his head. "If you don't drink, you'll dehydrate. We're not used to this heat."

Covid wiped his sweaty brow with his shirtsleeve, which was already drenched in perspiration. He nodded and accepted the canteen, removing his mask. "If this is what the days outside the bunker are like, we haven't been missing anything." He pointed to a grove of trees. "We can rest there. The trees will shade us from the sun."

Destine followed him into the grove. They were surprised to find a lake hidden behind the trees. "A pool of water!" Covid exclaimed. "I could use a bath to cool off and wash the sweat from my body. We can refill the canteens, too!" He stripped off his shirt and kicked off his shoes.

"Wait!" Destine cried. "Don't go near the water: it's polluted."

Covid paused. "How can you tell?"

She pointed toward the edge of the lake. "See the dead fish floating on top? There must be something contaminating the water that gradually kills them. It might not harm us immediately we don't want that touching our skin or inside us."

Covid stared longingly at the refreshing, inviting water. "Damn. All I want is to cool off." He pulled out his canteen and poured water down the back of his neck.

"Hey! That's our drinking water."

Covid recapped the canteen. "We'll find more. There's got to be drinkable water somewhere; otherwise, it doesn't matter how much I use. We can't survive out here if there's no water we can drink once our canteens run dry."

"Let's move on," Destine said. "This lake is too tempting."

Covid nodded. They replaced their facemasks and headed back out into the sun. They walked for miles, the unchanging scenery making it difficult to know how far they had traveled. Then, Covid espied something in the distance. "That structure... Is it a school or a church?"

Destine peered at it, squinting against the harsh rays of the sun. "Neither, I think. If it were a church it would have a spire. But it looks like there are other buildings clustered nearby. It could be a town. This rocky path we've been on may have been a road at one time."

"That means people... And food."

"Not necessarily. The virus may have killed everyone years ago. We could be walking into a ghost town."

"Even so, we might find something useful. If Corona and Kai came this way we might find some sign of them."

"Possibly, but don't get your hopes up."

Nonetheless, as they drew nearer Covid grew excited. "It *is* a town. It must be; look at all the structures." They walked through the center of the deserted street, taking in all the empty buildings on either side of them. Covid paused when he passed a glass window. "Look! We can see inside." He pressed his face against the window. "There are rows and rows stocked with tins like one of the storerooms in the bunker. We might find food or even water inside."

"This must be what they used to call a store or market. See if you can break down the door."

Covid approached the entrance and pressed against the door. "It wasn't locked." He pushed it open and stepped inside, followed by Destine. They wandered through the aisles, picking up various items from the shelves as they passed. "They have pictures on them. Do you think that's what's inside?"

"In most cases," Destine said, picking up a can. "This one has a picture of a ship. I doubt that's what's inside. Before the coronavirus, people used to sail ships on great bodies of water called seas and catch fish. There might be some sort of fish inside."

Covid frowned. "Do you think any of it would be edible after this long?"

"The tins in the bunker are. They were vacuum sealed. These look the same." Her eyes drifted to a plastic bag filled with candy. Destine ripped it open and, hesitatingly, lifted her facemask and placed one into her mouth. "Mmmm. Tastes fresh. Sweet. Try one."

Covid took one of the candies and sampled it. "Wow, that tastes good. Throw a couple bags into the sack." He perused the various items on the shelves. "If the rest of the stuff is safe to eat then we won't have to worry about provisions. Especially if there are more stores out there like this one." His eyes fell on a package of potato chips resting on a top shelf. He reached up to grab it, clutching the bottom of the bag. An arrow sliced through the air spearing the package and pinning it to the wall. Covid and Destine turned in surprise.

Two teenagers stood at the entrance aiming bows and arrows at them. Between them, a white-haired woman, her hair tied back in a bun, stood grinning. "Looks like we caught us someone raiding our stash," she said.

"They can't be Raiders 'cause we are, and we know all the other Raiders," the boy said. "They must be Utopians."

The woman shook her head. "Do they look like Utopians to you? 'Sides, Utopians wouldn't have the stones to come this far in."

The girl gleefully targeted Covid with her bow and arrow. "Can I shoot him now, Granny? Bet I can pierce his heart from here."

"Now Robin, what have I done taught you about meeting strangers?" Granny asked. "The first thing you do is find out their names. How else you gonna know what to write on the grave marker?"

The girl frowned, lowering her bow by a few degrees. "Yes, Granny." She looked up at Covid. "What's your name, boy?"

"Covid." He glanced cautiously at Destine. He whispered, "What do those psychology books say about this?"

"Covid," Robin repeated. "That's an odd name. You care how I spell it on the marker?"

"With a C," Destine said. "But I don't think you really want to shoot us."

Robin grinned. "I like shooting things. I'm real good at it."

"I bet you are," Destine said. "But I know how to help people who get sick or injured. I'm more useful alive than as a target."

"She's got a point there, Robin," Granny said. "Archer," she called out to the boy, "Don't shoot her."

Archer lowered his bow. "Shucks, Robin always gets to have all the fun."

"I take it you're her brother?" Destine asked.

"Yep, and just as good a shot, too. I could shoot you right between the eyes without budging from this doorframe."

Destine turned to Robin. "Are all the boys around here like your brother?"

Robin shrugged. "There ain't many our age, but yeah, I guess."

Destine gesture toward Covid. "Do you really want to kill the only new boy around?"

Robin lowered her bow. "Well, when you put it that way…" She stepped closer and perused his features. "He ain't too hard on the eyes." She turned back to the old lady. "Granny, can I keep him?"

She stroked her chin. "We'll see. We'll take them back with us. Now load up your sacks."

"We're looking for a girl and boy dressed like us."

"With them funny masks?" Granny asked. "Ain't seen 'em."

"Then, we'll be heading on," Covid said.

"Nope," Granny said. "You're coming back with us to the Outpost." She turned to Robin and Archer. "If they give you any trouble, shoot 'em."

Archer grinned. "Awesome."

Robin pouted. "You said I could keep him."

"Up to him if he wants to come home with us," Granny said. "Either way's fine with me; your brother could use the target practice."

Destine spoke up. "Of course we'll come back with you." She gave Covid an admonishing look.

"Yeah, sure," Covid said reluctantly. They watched Robin and Archer fill their sacks with canned goods. Then, the Raiders led them outside. Covid and Destine's eyes widened. "What are those things?"

Granny squinted at him. "What's wrong with you, boy? Ain't you never seen a horse before? You hop on back with Archer. Your girlfriend can ride with Robin."

"She's not my girlfriend," Covid said.

Robin grinned. "He can ride with me, Granny."

"He'll ride with your brother. Don't start getting' no ideas. Well, what are you two waitin' fer? Get up on them horses."

Archer reached down and offered Covid a hand up. Robin did the same for Destine. "Hold on tight," Granny said, as each wrapped their arms around the riders' waists. "Giddyap!" The three horses galloped off.

Chapter Five

CORALIE SAT IN AN ARMCHAIR in the corner of the social area reading a book. She had grown tired of staring at the four walls of her small quarters and she had felt the room — the size of a walk-in closet — becoming increasingly claustrophobic. Coralie thought by sitting at the far end of the designated social area she would be relieved of any obligation to actually be sociable. She pressed her nose into the book as Dax approached as if to drive home the point.

"Hey, loser," Dax said. "Whatcha reading?"

Coralie slid the book below her nose, glancing up at Dax. "I have a name, you know."

Dax shrugged. "A dumb one at that. Whoever tagged you with it must have known what a loser you'd turn out to be."

Coralie sneered at her. "Go quarantine yourself." She tossed the book at Dax and rushed from the social area. Dax picked up the book and took her place in the armchair.

Keiana watched the exchange but said nothing. Her gaze fell on Lucian, who was continually scribbling on a notepad before ripping out each sheet, crumpling it into a ball, and tossing it to the floor. "You know we have a finite amount of paper."

The 13-year-old boy looked up. "We have reams and reams of it in one of the storerooms. Besides, I'm the only one who ever uses it."

"Working on another song?"

Lucian nodded. "I can't seem to get the lyrics right."

"It doesn't have to be perfect."

"Yes, it does. That's the whole point. Why do you think everyone goes around singing my songs? It's because the lyrics are meaningful. If I'm to create something of enduring value then it has to be perfect."

"That's an awful large burden for a 13-year-old to carry," Keiana said.

"You don't understand. I have more creativity and imagination than any of the others. That's my special talent. It's what makes me… Me. It sets me apart from anyone else and makes me important even though I'm one of the youngest. And because I'm so young, no one will take me seriously unless every song I compose is absolutely perfect."

Keiana pondered his words. "You may be right about that. Your songs do have the ability to move people. You're able to make people see and feel things they might not otherwise. That *is* a very special talent… And a great responsibility."

"Responsibility? What do you mean?"

Keiana gave him a knowing look, which was anything but to him. "Use as much paper as you wish."

Before he could reply, their conversation was interrupted by Tristan, who tossed a basketball to Lucian. "Dude! I've got the basketball hoop set up in the exercise room. Come on."

Chapter Five

Lucian tossed it back. "Can't. Busy right now. I'm working on a song."

Tristan frowned. "You're always working on a song. That stuff can wait. I'm talking about having fun. You know, carpe diem — seize the day!"

Lucian shook his head. "Some other time." He returned to his scribbling.

Tristan turned to Keiana. "I hate it when he gets like this." He held up the basketball. "I don't suppose you'd..." He paused. "Never mind."

A hush fell over the social area as Varian entered flanked by two of the older boys and followed by Blaine and Esme. Varian scanned their faces. "At least some of you are all in one place. It occurred to me I need to have a way to speak to everyone at once so I've decided everyone will meet here each morning before breakfast and again after dinner."

"Why do we need meetings twice a day?" Tristan asked.

"If we don't need a meeting then I'll simply say no meeting today but it's difficult to get everyone together and I'll have a few announcements to make. For example, tomorrow morning I'll be announcing the new schedule of chores."

"Why do we need a new schedule?" Dax asked.

"I've had to reallocate some of chores. With my new duties as leader I won't have time to do my chores so I'm dividing them among some of the younger kids. The same's true for the chores of several of the older boys, including my new enforcers, Arlo and Nico." He gestured to the two brawny, older boys on either side of him.

Keiana frowned. "Enforcers?"

"I had to give them a title," Varian said. "They'll be in charge of enforcing the new rules. We do want everything to run smoothly, don't we?"

"What new rules?" Dax asked.

"You'll find out when I announce them. In the meantime, spread the word about tonight's meeting. Fifteen minutes after dinner. See you then." Varian turned and left with his enforcers, Esme, and Blaine in tow.

Tristan glanced at Keiana. "That was—"

"Ominous?" she asked.

"I was going to say weird but that works, too."

Dax frowned. "He can't just dump his chores — and those of his buddies — onto the rest of us."

Keiana shrugged. "You did elect him leader. I'm more interested in hearing about these new rules Varian intends to introduce tonight." Keiana pondered what Varian might be planning.

Fiona knocked on the doorframe of Nessa's quarters. Her door was open and Nessa looked up. "May I come in?"

"Sure."

Fiona noticed the younger girl had an array of crayons scattered across her bed and was drawing with one. "What are you doing?"

"I'm making Welcome Home posters for Corona, Kai, Covid, and Destine. I'm going to color them and then we can hang them in the social area when they return."

Fiona gulped. "That's sweet, hun, and very thoughtful of you but you realize they might not be coming back?"

"Of course they'll be back. That's why Covid and Destine went out after them."

"Yes, that's true," Fiona said, treading carefully so as not to shatter the rosy optimism conjured from Nessa's naïveté. "But there's always the possibility something could happen to them. You know it's extremely dangerous to be outside the bunker."

40

Chapter Five

Nessa smiled. "They'll be fine. Things are going to be good again. You'll see."

Varian led Esme into his quarters. He turned to his pair of enforcers. "Go. I'll summon you if I need you." The two large boys turned and left. "See how they obey unhesitatingly? I've bought their loyalty for the price of a few promises."

Esme reclined in his bed. "Now come and purchase mine."

"In good time. I must prepare for tonight's meeting." He turned to close the door and saw Blaine still standing in the doorway. "What are you doing here?"

"When you dismissed the enforcers, I didn't think you meant for me to go, too. I could help you prepare."

Varian heard the neediness and enthusiasm in Blaine's voice. He knew an unfilled need represented an opportunity. "You don't like them, do you?"

"Who?"

"My new enforcers."

Chagrined, Blaine turned away. "They... They haven't always treated me well. They're bullies. Arlo and Nico think just because they're older and bigger than me they can pick on me." He looked down. "Once they even pushed my face into the latrine."

Varian arched an eyebrow. "Have they picked on you recently?"

Blaine shook his head.

"I'll have a word with them to make sure they know you serve me and as such they must do whatever you say. Would you like that?"

A wide grin appeared slowly on Blaine's face as he realized what Varian was offering. "I can boss Arlo and Nico around and they have to follow my orders?"

"If they wish to remain enforcers. They're lucky to have been chosen for what will soon become a coveted position."

"You don't mind that they're bullies?"

"On the contrary, I find that a positive attribute — as long as they're *my* bullies. And since they're mine, you needn't fear them." Varian contemplated. "Would you like them to address you as *sir*?"

Blaine grinned. "That'd be awesome!"

"There is one important job you could do for me," Varian said.

"Anything!" Blaine exclaimed. "Is it really important?"

"Absolutely essential," Varian said as if reeling in a fish. "I want you to mingle with the others. Listen to what your friends say and become friends with everyone else. People will say things about me to each other that they wouldn't say to my face. Your job will be to listen and report back to me what they truly think and say."

Blaine cocked his head. "You want me to rat out my friends?"

"I want you to help me, your friend, keep everyone safe. I expect there'll be some who plot against me and I need a heads-up. You'd be helping me and therefore our entire society. It's a very important role I'm asking you to play." He paused, for dramatic effect. "Of course, if you think it's too much responsibility or you'd rather not be involved…"

"No, no. I definitely want to be involved. Let me help. Just tell me what to do. I'll do anything you want."

Varian smiled. "For now, just keep your ears to the ground. Now get to work. Esme and I have things to.. discuss."

Blaine nodded enthusiastically and dashed off. Varian locked the door behind him.

"Paranoid much?" Esme asked.

"Just because you're paranoid doesn't mean they're not out to get you. Or soon will be. I'm bringing a new order to the bunker. Change means there'll be winners and losers, and losers tend to be resentful. Blaine will be an excellent bloodhound to ferret out any discontent that could rise to the level of a threat."

"You handled him masterfully." She slipped off her clothes. "Now do the same to me."

The social area had emptied as most prepared for dinner. Only a few stragglers remained, including Dax and Lucian, the latter still hard at work. Dax picked up one of the discarded balls of paper wadded up on the floor and unfurled it. She shook her head reading it. "You're never going to find a word to rhyme with orange."

Lucian glanced up with an annoyed look. "Go away."

Dax shrugged and walked off, re-crumpling the paper into a ball and tossing it at Lucian.

Corbin caught up to her. "I don't know why you'd waste your time talking to him."

"Get lost, Corbin."

"Friendly as ever, huh Dax? I think it's your warmth and compassion that draws me to you. What is it about me that you like?"

Dax stared him in the eyes. "Absolutely nothing. You're a slimy maggot."

"That's what I like most about you: your honesty. Most people hide what they really feel and only say what they think others want to hear, But not you, Dax. No, you don't care what anyone thinks of you; you say whatever's on your mind regardless of whom you offend. Yet even so, you're not completely transparent. There's a part of you I don't understand." He perused her features with a cold, calculating stare.

"What do you want, Corbin?"

Corbin shrugged. "Who says I want anything?"

Dax sneered. "The only reason you talk to anyone is because you want something from them."

"Maybe I simply want to be friends."

Dax laughed. "You don't know the meaning of the word. You'd first have to have feelings and emotions. You may fool the others but not me. The only thing you're interested in is yourself."

Corbin smiled. "As I said, that's what I like about you. That, and the fact you're smart. Oh, I don't mean book smart like Destine or Keiana. You're savvy. It's almost like a special gene that gives survivors like us the edge. You sense it too, don't you?"

"Sense what?"

"Change. There's uncertainty in the air. Life's about to shift dramatically and I need to calculate how to turn these events to my advantage. We view the world through the same lens; if not friends, we should at least be allies."

"Alliances requires trust — a quality not inspired by a liar and petty thief."

"Then call it a detente — an alliance built on mutual necessity rather than trust. We studied those in history class, remember?"

"The Americans and the Soviets — two rival Cold War superpowers that cooperated on the first joint space mission."

"You were always a good student. We may not be friends but we each possess skills the others don't that will help us survive whatever changes are coming our way. It only makes sense that we cooperate."

Dax frowned. "We'll see." She turned and headed off to dinner.

The after-dinner crowd filled the social area. Varian, staring out at the sea of faces, looked pleased to see a standing room audience. "I hope you all enjoyed your dinner. As you know, food is one of our most important resources in the bunker. Fortunately, the bunker was well-stocked with vacuum-sealed cans of food and our hydroponic garden has been extremely productive even using artificial lighting. But I've examined our reserves and I see that we're consuming them at a rapid rate so we'll have to invoke some form of rationing to make our food last."

"We never had rationing before," Dax said.

"True," Varian said, "and that was negligent of our previous leader. His mismanagement has placed us in this dire situation. He was so concerned with the present that he neglected to prepare for the future. Fortunately for all of you, I take my leadership responsibilities extremely seriously. After all, I did promise to keep you safe."

"What sort of rationing are you talking about?" Fiona asked.

"That will be up to each individual," Varian replied. "Everyone will be issued a certain number of credits each day that they can spend on food or other commodities."

"What are credits?" Nessa asked.

"In this case, we'll be using casino chips. We found a box of them in one of the storage bins. I've moved it to a secure location, of course. The chips are in denominations of one, five, ten, twenty, and fifty. Eventually, you'll be able to use your credits to buy all sorts of goods and services."

Keiana cocked her head. "You're establishing an economy — like those we studied in our classes."

"All societies that we've read about have had some form of economy. We should've established this in the bunker years ago. Of course, we were only children then. Now that we've matured we must take steps to build a proper society. Don't you agree, Keiana?"

Everything Varian said made sense yet Keiana felt uncomfortable. Nonetheless, she was forced to agree, thereby publicly validating his actions. "It does make sense," she replied reluctantly.

"I'm glad you agree. Here's how it'll work: everyday, each thirteen-year-old will receive one credit; the fourteen-year-olds two credits; the fifteen-year-olds three credits; the sixteen-year-olds four credits; the seventeen-year-olds five credits; the eighteen-year-olds six credits; and the nineteen-year-olds seven credits."

"That's not fair!" Nessa exclaimed. "Everyone should get the same amount."

"Why Nessa," Varian replied gesturing to his two enforcers. "Look at Nico and Arlo. Surely you realize big husky nineteen-year-old boys eat far more food than delicate little girls like yourself. Obviously those who are bigger and older require more food."

"That's true but it's still not fair," Nessa said.

"She's right," Fiona said.

Esme stepped forward. "Varian's looking out for our welfare and all you can do is attack him. There's nothing to stop you or any of the older kids from sharing your credits with the younger ones or using your credit allowance to buy food for them."

"Yeah," Blaine said. "At least Varian's come up with a plan to keep us from starving to death when the food runs out. You should be praising Leader Varian instead of criticizing him."

Fiona nodded. "You're right. I'm sorry. After all, we did elect you to make difficult decisions and that must not be easy."

"Leader Varian?" Keiana asked.

"Blaine suggested the person in charge of running the bunker have a title and I agreed. A position as important as that should have a title after all, shouldn't it?"

Again, Keiana felt uncomfortable but couldn't dispute his logic.

"Now then, if you'll all line up, Blaine will distribute your first day's credits." It wasn't possible to form a straight line within the crowded social area but the teenagers arranged themselves in an orderly fashion. Varian smiled. It had been a good day.

Chapter Six

Kai opened his eyes. The first thing he noticed was the light. Not quite daylight, as he and Corona had become used to recently, but more like the artificial light of the bunker. The thought of Corona made him try to bolt up but he discovered he couldn't move. He felt cold metal press against his wrists and ankles as he attempted to sit up and he realized he was securely shackled to a table. "Corona!" he called out.

"Don't shout," Corona called back to him. "I'm right behind you. Are you bound to a table, too?"

"Yeah. Where are we?"

"No clue. I woke up ten minutes ago staring at the ceiling."

"I suppose you also have no idea how we got here or why we're locked down?"

"All I know is someone did this to us. That means there are other people alive — and we've found them."

"More like they've found us." Kai tugged at the metal clamps. "It's no use. I can't break free."

They heard a door creak open, followed by the sound of footsteps. The head of a middle-aged man hovered above them, temporarily blocking the fluorescent light. "I trust you've had a pleasant nap," he said.

"Where are we?" Corona asked. "Who are you?"

"More importantly, let us go," Kai said.

"Of course. You were only restrained so you wouldn't injure yourselves during your medical examinations. Now that you're awake, there's no reason to keep you restrained." He pressed a lever on each of the tables and the shackles opened.

Kai and Corona sat up, massaging their aching wrists. "You haven't answered our questions," Corona said.

"All in good time. I'm sure you have many questions and I'll do my best to answer them all. But first, are you hungry? We've prepared a meal waiting for you in our dining room. If you'll follow me."

Kai glanced at Corona as they tacitly exchanged the conclusion they had no choice but to follow him. They each hopped off their respective examination tables and followed him out of the room. As they walked down the hallway it became apparent they were in a luxurious mansion like the ones they had seen in some of the picture books in the bunker's library. The building was spacious and the halls were lined with paintings and tapestries. They were led into a room with a magnificent chandelier and beneath it a large mahogany dining table with eight ornate cushioned chairs around it.

"Please, be seated."

There were two plates set at the table, several platters of vegetables, and a large platter of beef. A pitcher containing an iced liquid also sat on the table, as did two glasses filled with the same liquid. Corona looked hesitatingly at Kai.

"Come now, we haven't poisoned the food. We had ample opportunity to kill you had we wished."

His logic made sense, so Corona and Kai sat and began eating. "This beef doesn't taste like our canned food," Kai said.

"Canned?" the man asked. "Certainly not. Our beef is fresh and the vegetables are harvested daily from our gardens. Now, I believe you had some questions."

Corona swallowed her food and asked, "Who are you and how did we get here?"

"My name is Proctor. One of our patrols found you outside the city. You were both unconscious; they thought you dead at first. You were badly dehydrated and had suffered heatstroke but appeared otherwise healthy. Rather than leave you to die, they brought you back here."

Kai washed down his food with a sip of the drink and then asked, "Where's here?"

"This used to be a rather exclusive neighborhood in what was once a small city before the plague. When the coronavirus appeared, we were unprepared. Thousands died. But most survived. We thought we had gone through hell and lived to come back and tell the tale. We didn't realize the virus would return in a second, and far more deadly, wave. It decimated the planet's population. When it was over, a little more than eight hundred of us had survived in the entire city."

"The virus is gone?" Kai asked.

"We haven't seen any trace of it. We tested you for it, of course, but you're both clean. We devised a vaccine after surviving the second wave so we believe we're immune to it. We moved from our homes and consolidated ourselves in this neighborhood. This was once an area of great wealth:

luxurious homes and mansions were sitting vacant, save for the dead bodies of their former owners. There's an old saying, 'To the victors go the spoils.' We had conquered the virus and survived; it was only fitting we should reward ourselves. We built a geodesic dome to wall off the neighborhood, which became our new city of Utopia."

"Where are the others?" Corona asked.

"In their homes. Only the patrols leave the city; everyone else stays within the dome."

"What are they patrolling for?" Corona asked.

"Raiders. At first we thought you might be Raiders, but your medical exams showed no trace of any antibodies within you."

"Antibodies?" Kai asked.

Proctor nodded. "The Raiders who survived the plague were all exposed. You're lucky we came across you first. The Raiders are savage killers. We're constantly on guard against their attacks. They want our supplies and anything else they might get their hands on. Fortunately, the dome keeps them out and our patrols prevent them from coming too close to Utopia. Are you enjoying your dinner?"

"I'll say!" Kai exclaimed. "I don't think I've ever eaten this well before."

"I'm pleased your meal is satisfactory."

Kai nodded enthusiastically. "More than satisfactory: delicious."

"If I may now pose a question to you," Proctor said. "If you're not Raiders, then what are you and where did you come from?"

Corona opened her mouth to speak but Kai shot her warning glance and interrupted. "We come from far away. We were exploring and got lost. I doubt we could tell you where our home is in relation to Utopia."

Chapter Six

"Then, I trust you'll think of Utopia as your new home. We have a civilized society with a moral code of conduct."

"A code?" Corona repeated. "We follow one, as well."

"How interesting," Proctor said. "I'd like to hear more of it at a later date. But for now, I have work to return to. We've prepared separate quarters for you both; later, you may choose one of the vacant homes as your own. We'll speak more in the morning. Please, follow me to your rooms."

Proctor led Corona and Kai from the dining room down a long hallway and deposited them at the doors of two adjoining rooms. Corona was shocked at how large the bedroom was. It was easily a dozen times the size of her small room in the bunker. It had a dresser with a huge mirror and an enormous plush bed with a soft down comforter. She ran to the bed and jumped onto it, reveling in the luxury.

Proctor, meanwhile, continued down the hall of the mansion and entered the study. A middle-aged woman in a white lab coat was waiting for him. "Dr. Carstairs. You have the rest of the exam results?" he asked.

"Yes. The specimens are in excellent health. I don't believe either of them has ever been sick a day in their lives. Apparently they were vaccinated against major diseases in early childhood and not exposed to any since."

"And the boy?"

"A superb specimen. Unquestionably virile, given his youthful age. His sperm count is off the charts. When do you want him transferred?"

"In the morning. I think he should have a good night's sleep. He has a busy day ahead of him and I want him in top form."

Dr. Carstairs nodded, "And the girl?"

"Give me a report on what organs she has that are ripe for harvesting. They can be removed tomorrow and then ship her remains to the farm."

"Certainly. We can schedule the organ removal for the afternoon."

"Excellent. My only regret is we have no idea where they came from or if there are more of them. But one should never look a gift horse in the mouth."

Corona was still asleep when Proctor knocked on Kai's bedroom door. The boy woke up and opened the door.

"Good morning," Proctor said. "Did you have a good night's rest?"

Kai grinned. "I slept like a baby. That bed's softer than what I'm used to."

"Excellent. We want you to be happy while you're in Utopia. If you'll come with me, I have something to show you."

"What about Corona?"

"Let her sleep. I'm sure she needs her rest after your journey. This only concerns you."

Kai followed Proctor down the hall. "How so?"

"Utopia desperately needs your assistance. You may recall yesterday I explained how we had devised a vaccine against the coronavirus."

"Yes. That's quite an achievement."

"Our scientists worked day and night, as their friends and family fell victim to the virus. As soon as we had a working vaccine, we administered it immediately to the city's entire remaining population. It was literally a matter of life and death. Normally, such a vaccine would have undergone months or even years of testing to discover any side effects, however we lacked the luxury of time."

"But obviously it worked."

They came to the drawing room where Dr. Carstairs was waiting with a half-dozen attractive young women. "The virus had already killed off eighty percent of the older population and twenty percent of the younger population. As a result, two-thirds of our survivors were children who have since grown into young adults. Utopia has nearly three hundred young women of childbearing age on whom we must rely to continue our heritage. Unfortunately, our vaccine had an unintended side effect: it rendered all of our men infertile. We can't repopulate Utopia; at least, not without outside assistance. Until your arrival, the only fertile males were Raiders and it was the rare encounter that left any alive."

Kai cocked his head. "Are you suggesting what I think you are?"

"These are some of Utopia's young women whose fondest dream is motherhood. An impossible dream without a fertile male like yourself. On behalf of all Utopia's young women they wanted to tell you how grateful they would be for your help in impregnating them." The young women smiled at Kai.

Kai grinned like a hyena in heat. "This place just keeps getting better and better. Should we go back into the bedroom to get started?"

"You can stay here," Proctor said. "I'll ask the girls to step outside so you may change into this robe. Hand Dr. Carstairs your clothes and she'll take care of them."

"You bet!" He tossed her his clothes as he removed them, which she neatly folded and placed in a cabinet. When Kai had changed into the robe, Proctor gestured for him to sit in what appeared to be an examination chair. "Not another medical exam?" Kai asked. "Can't we do this part later?"

"This won't take long," Proctor said. "Let Dr. Carstairs strap you in." She tightened the leather straps around his wrists. "Lift your legs into these stirrups," Proctor said, as Dr. Carstairs strapped in Kai's ankles.

"He's securely strapped in," Dr. Carstairs said.

"Excellent," Proctor replied.

"Do I get to choose the girls?" Kai asked.

Proctor chuckled. "Oh, you won't see them again. They simply wanted to thank you for your generous donation."

Kai cocked his head. "Donation?"

"As I explained yesterday, Utopia is a civilized society. Surely you didn't think we would condone sex outside of marriage? That would go against our moral code."

"But the fertilization?"

"Don't worry, that will all be accomplished through artificial insemination," Proctor said, as Dr. Carstairs rolled in a machine. Proctor spread his hands. "The Dairy is set up for just that purpose. We call this machine the milker, similar to what farmers used to use on cows — but modified for humans, of course. We calculate we should have enough sperm to inseminate all of Utopia's childbearing-aged women in six months if we keep you hooked up for eight hours each day."

Kai became agitated. "Wait a minute! You're not putting that contraption on me!"

"Relax and try not to moo… I mean move," Proctor said. "I wouldn't want you to hurt yourself." He walked over to a record player and turned it on. "The generators provide limited power but they do allow us one of our luxuries:

classical music. I trust you'll find Wagner's 'Ride of the Valkyries' appropriate. It's a work that begins with intense upward violin swoops, followed by the cellos playing an almost constant rhythm that builds to a rousing climax." The vibrant classical music filled the air. "It's set for continuous play. I'll see you in eight hours." He motioned to Dr. Carstairs and they both left the room.

"Come back!" Kai screamed. Get this off of me! Help!" The rising allegro of the violin, English horn, oboe, and clarinets drowned out his cries.

It was a soft, gentle noise yet Corona nonetheless heard it through her slumber. She slowly opened her eyes to determine its source. As she focused, she saw a figure hovering at the edge of her bed. She jumped up. "Who are you?"

"I'm sorry; I didn't mean to wake you," the young woman said. On closer inspection, Corona could see she was wiping the dresser top with a cloth and had knocked over a music box. "I'm Maga, the cleaner. Please, go back to sleep."

"How did you get in? I tried the door last night and it was locked."

"I have keys to all the rooms, else I wouldn't be able to do my daily cleaning. Proctor told me not to disturb you; I'm ever so sorry."

Corona rose from the bed. "That's all right. I normally don't sleep this late. It must have been the comfortable mattress and the delicious dinner last night."

"Yes, we just got a fresh shipment of meat from the farm yesterday. It tastes best when it's fresh from the slaughterhouse."

"The farm? Is that where you raise cattle? I've read about that in books."

Maga chuckled. "There haven't been any cattle around here since before the plague. No animals at all, except horses and the wild wolves but they can't get into the dome. The farm's just outside the dome so we don't have to smell the odors from the slaughterhouse."

Corona nodded. "Have you seen my friend Kai? Is he awake yet?"

"I haven't seen him but I heard his voice when I was cleaning down the hall near the drawing room. A bit hard to hear over the music, though. You must be awfully proud of him."

"Proud?"

"He's going to help us become mothers."

Corona laughed. "Well, he does act childish at times, but I don't think he needs mothering. Wait, you said there aren't any animals around. Where does your meat that you butcher at the farm come from?"

"It's terribly dangerous outside the dome. We send out constant armed patrols because we fear the Raiders will try to break in and take our supplies. They're jealous of the luxury we have in Utopia. When the patrols capture or kill them, they bring them back to Utopia. Obviously the dead men can't produce the fluid Dr. Carstairs needs — and even the living men can't make much of it anymore — so they're taken to the farm."

A puzzled look appeared on Corona's face. "But why? Do you cremate their bodies there or..." A horrible thought crossed her mind. "The slaughterhouse!"

"They chop 'em up at the farm, wrap 'em into chunks, and deliver them here, nice and neat. Each one can make several meals."

Chapter Six

"The dinner last night..." Corona felt the bile rising from her stomach. She started gagging and vomiting, frightening Maga.

"What's wrong? Are you ill?" Maga became frantic, uncertain what to do. "Stay calm. I'll go get Dr. Carstairs." The frightened young woman raced from the room.

Corona forced herself to stop vomiting. She saw the door that had kept her locked in the room during the night now swinging wide open. *I've got to find Kai and tell him,* she thought. *We've got to get out of this place.* She ran out of the bedroom, pausing at the doorway. *She said Kai was in the drawing room. Where—?* Corona heard loud music coming from down the hall. "Maga said she heard music from the room where Kai was." She followed the sound and entered the drawing room.

Chapter Seven

COVID AND DESTINE HELD ONTO the horse-riding teens for dear life, terrified as they surrendered all control to the galloping beasts and their masters. For their part, Archer and Robin enjoyed the air blasting their faces as the horses raced across the landscape. As he watched the scenery recede into the background, Covid said, "We certainly do cover a lot of territory fast on these things."

"They ain't got horses where you're from?" Archer asked.

"No, I've never seen one before. Where do they come from?"

"They've always been around, at least that's what Granny says. Most animals was immune to the virus. You don't see many around, though. Granny says they went off lookin' fer food. The horses gots plenty of grazing room so they stuck around and the wolves hunt their own food, like rabbits and other critters."

"Are there a lot of you Raiders?"

"Sure, but they're scattered. Raiders ain't organized like Utopians. If we was, we'd be too easy to wipe out. Instead, there's pockets of Raiders spread out all over. That store you was in is our stash; other Raiders know to steer clear of it 'less'en they want trouble."

"Sorry, we didn't know."

"Yeah, I done sussed that already. Glad I didn't shoot you back there; it's nice to have someone new to talk to."

"You make those flying things yourself?"

"The arrows? Shucks, yeah. We ain't got fancy rifles like the Utopians but you can kill a man just as quick with a bow and arrow. I don't know how many rifles them Utopians got stored away but I reckon one day they're gonna run out of bullets but we'll still be able to make plenty of arrows from what nature gives us."

The importance of being able to create weapons from a ubiquitous supply of natural materials in the environment resonated with Covid. "Can you teach me how to make them?"

Archer grinned. "Sure, it's easy. I can show you how to make a fishing pole, too."

"I thought the water was contaminated."

"Nah, just certain spots. You gotta know which ones is safe is all."

The remnants of a small mobile home trailer park came into view. "Archer, Robin, tie up the horses," Granny said. "I'll let the others know these two are with us." She turned to Destine. "Wouldn't want you gettin' shot by mistake on your first day."

"What is this place?" Destine asked.

"We call it the Outpost. The patrols don't come this far out." Granny pulled out a container of snuff and sniffed the smokeless tobacco. She smiled as she inhaled. "Good soil out here; we grow the tobacco leaves ourselves." Granny gestured. "All this used to be filled with families before the plague. Some of them was annoying but I miss them all now."

Destine's eyes widened. "You lived here before the virus? You remember what life was like?"

"'Course I do. A dozen years ain't that long ago. 'Course, it must seem that way to Archer and Robin; they's only toddlers at the time. The virus took their parents but spared me, Lord knows why. Mysterious ways and all, I reckon. Disease don't discriminate: white or black, rich or poor. The virus was the great equalizer. Even them rich folks in that there domed city died gasping fer their last breath like the rest of us."

Covid looked around the remains of the trailer park. "Is this it? Is this all of humanity that's left?"

Granny laughed. "Hell boy, this ain't nothing but what's left of one small city in one state in one country on a very big planet. Used to be you could get on an airplane and travel from one end of the country to another, or simply flip on a television set, and see what was happening in other places. Not no more. The plague done changed that. Ain't no way to know what's happening elsewhere. No phones, no television, no internet; heck, we ain't even got no freaking electricity 'less'en you can score a working generator. But I reckon there's folks what survived out there, same as us. You do what you have to, to survive. I done things I never would've dreamed of doing before the plague."

Covid ruminated. "I was too young to remember life before the plague. Was it really that different?"

"Like night and day. Back then, I'd have been ashamed of a lot of what I done. Not now, though. I'm proud of them things 'cause if I hadn't done 'em, Archer and Robin wouldn't be alive today. In them days, I'd have baked you a cherry pie and tucked you into bed at night; but now, if'n I thought you was a threat to Archer and Robin, I'd kill you without any hesitation."

"We're not a threat to them."

Granny nodded. "That's why you're still breathing." She walked over to a large metal bell attached to a pole and rang it. Eight men and women Granny's age stepped out of their aluminum shelters. "This here's Covid and Destine. They're friends, so don't go killing them."

Covid and Destine gave a slight wave. Surveying the new arrivals, Destine asked, "Are Archer and Robin the only kids at the Outpost?"

Granny nodded. "A lot of the other outposts have kids; those who were teenagers when the plague struck are in their late twenties now. A lot of them don't want to bring children into this world. Can't say I blame them. This used to be a retirement community. My daughter and her husband came with their kids to stay after they lost their home."

"How did that happen?" Destine asked.

"The economic collapse during the first outbreak of the virus. Folks was told to stay inside. Businesses failed, folks had no income and the banks foreclosed on their homes... fat lot of good that done them money grubbers in the end. Funny thing: it turns out if you take people's jobs and their homes, they ain't gonna need no banks. Anyway, they done moved in with me so they was here when the second wave hit. As you can see, a few of us older folk survived but most didn't."

"So Archer and Robin's parents were killed in the second wave of the virus?" Destine asked. "I didn't know there had been a second wave."

Granny squinted at her. "Everyone knows that, even if it was before they was born. You been living under a rock, girl?"

Destine thought back to the underground bunker they had been raised in. "You could say something like that."

Archer and Robin came running back. "Come on," Archer said. "I'm gonna teach you how to make a fishing pole and catch fish."

Robin reached for Destine's hand. "And I'm gonna show you how to make bows and arrows and teach you how to shoot." The four teens ran off. Granny watched, amazed at the rare excitement and enthusiasm Archer and Robin were displaying.

The music was even louder when Corona entered the drawing room. Kai's cries distracted her. "Help!"

She saw Kai strapped to the chair and ran to him. "Kai! What—?"

"Unplug that machine!" He grunted, his body arching against the leather straps restraining him.

Corona saw a cable leading from the milker to a portable generator. She tugged on the cord and the milker ceased functioning.

Kai sighed, his body collapsing into the chair, limp and exhausted. "Untie me," he gasped.

Corona unstrapped his wrists. "These people are monsters. We have to get out of here."

"Really?" Kai asked, untying his ankle straps. "What was your first clue?"

"I'll tell you later. I don't have my facemask; let's find our masks and leave."

65

Kai jumped up, covering himself with the robe. "Facemasks? "I don't have my pants." He opened the cabinet he had seen Dr. Carstairs place his clothes in and quickly dressed. "I don't think we need masks if the virus has been gone for years. The real question is, how we get out of the dome?"

"We ask for directions." Corona saw eight feet of plastic tubing coming from the milker and ripped it out. "Follow me." She led Kai back to her room, where Maga was pleading with Dr. Carstairs.

"She was terribly ill. I didn't realize I had left the door open."

"You fool! She could be anywhere. I'll deal with you later. Now I have to sound the alarm and—" Dr. Carstairs felt the plastic tubing slip around her neck from behind her and tighten.

"Show us the way out," Corona said, "if you want to keep breathing." She pulled the tubing tighter. Dr. Carstairs nodded while trying to grasp the tubing around her neck. Corona called out to Maga. "Give my sack to Kai." Maga nodded and quickly handed Corona's sack to Kai. Corona ushered Dr. Carstairs out the door. "Lock it," Corona said. "Lock Maga inside and then show us how to exit the dome."

Dr. Carstairs did as she was instructed. "You won't get away. We're miles from anywhere else and once you're outside the dome, the patrols will hunt you down."

Corona ignored her comment. "Which way?"

Reluctantly, Dr. Carstairs led them to an exit. "Surrender now and I promise your death will be painless."

Corona tightened her grip on the plastic tubing, watching stoically as Dr. Carstairs struggled to rip the tubing from her neck as she gasped and turned blue. Gradually, her struggling ceased and she slumped against the wall into unconsciousness.

"You killed her!" Kai exclaimed.

"No, she's breathing. I cut off her oxygen long enough to make her unconscious. When she wakes up, every Utopian in this dome will be after us."

Kai glanced outside the exit. "She was right; we won't get far on foot." He gestured out the doorway. "See that huge tree over there?"

Corona nodded.

"I'm going to climb up it. Once I'm hidden on a branch, when you see a patrol coming run out to the tree and stand beneath it. Surrender to the patrol but make them come out of their vehicle to capture you."

"Getting captured? That's your plan?"

"Trust me. It's the only plan we've got." Kai raced out to the tree.

Corona started leisurely walking toward the tree. She wondered how long it would take for Dr. Carstairs to regain consciousness and sound the alarm. She didn't have long to wait. She heard sirens coming from the building behind her. In the distance, Corona saw a Humvee headed toward her. She ran beneath the tree and froze.

The gunner looked down from the turret. "Put your hands up." He hopped out of the Humvee and approached her. Corona pretended to faint, dropping to the ground. The gunner called back to the driver, "Come out here and give me a hand." The driver stepped out of the Humvee and joined the gunner beneath the tree. Kai dropped from the tree limb landing atop the driver, stunning him. The gunner turned at the sound. Kai jumped up and slugged him. He hit him three more times until the gunner collapsed, unconscious. The driver rose to his knees preparing to stand but Corona picked up a heavy rock and smashed it on his head.

"What now?" Corona asked.

Kai pointed to the Humvee. "We've got a ride out of here."

They climbed inside. "You know how to operate this?" Corona asked.

"If it's what I think it is. It looks like some kind of car. I've read all about sports cars. You turn them on with a key in the ignition."

"What's the ignition?"

"Um, it's a guy thing. You wouldn't understand."

"You don't know either, huh? Doesn't matter; I don't see any keys."

"There has to be one."

Corona glanced at the dashboard. "What about that lever that says 'Eng Stop,' 'Run,' and 'Start'?"

Kai looked up at the lever on the left side of the dashboard. He flipped to the next position, labeled 'Run'. A button lit up. "Nothing's happening." He flipped the lever to the last position, marked 'Start'. The engine turned over. Kai smiled and pointed to a rod sticking up. "That's the gearshift: I know how to do this part." Kai placed the Humvee in Drive and stepped on the accelerator, pressing it to the floor. The vehicle shot forward in a burst of speed, throwing Kai and Corona against the seat. "Whoa!"

"It's working!" Corona exclaimed. "We're leaving Utopia far behind. You can slow down."

"I'm not sure how to do that. But I figured out how to steer it so we won't crash into anything."

"Do you know how to stop it?" Corona asked anxiously.

"I think it'll stop if I take my foot off the accelerator. At least, that's how cars are supposed to work."

"How far can we go before this thing runs out of power?"

"I'm sure it was fully powered since it was about to go on patrol."

"What does it use as a power source? Look out for that tree!"

Kai swerved the wheel. "I've got it. This is actually fun. Most cars ran on a fluid called gasoline but some ran on batteries. But I've never seen a picture of a car that looked like this."

Corona felt under her seat. "I think I found the battery."

"Good, we can recharge it if we can find a generator. I wonder how far this will take us?"

"Probably only as far as the Utopia patrols normally go, unless they have a recharging station."

"If they do, we don't know where it is. We could charge it using the bunker's generators."

Corona shook her head. "That would mean going back. I want to see the rest of this world first. When it runs out of power, we'll make note of where we left it so one day we can come back for it." She turned to Kai. "What were they doing to you back there?"

Kai gulped and instinctively covered his crotch. "Um, torture. But I didn't tell them anything about the bunker."

Corona nodded. "It looked quite… painful."

Kai winced. "Can we change the subject? And promise me you won't mention this to anyone. Besides, I'm getting hungry. We should look for something to eat."

Corona cringed. "Yeah, about that…"

Chapter Eight

MAGA WAS FRIGHTENED. IT HAD been hours since Corona had forced Dr. Carstairs to lock her inside what had been Corona's guest bedroom in Utopia and Maga had no idea what had become of either Corona or Dr. Carstairs. All she knew was that she was in trouble. How much trouble remained to be seen.

Maga thought she had done the right thing. After all, she knew the strangers were valuable and it made sense to rush for Dr. Carstairs when she had observed Corona vomiting in spasms. If only she hadn't left the door open. She knew Dr. Carstairs to be a cold and vindictive woman and the last time she had seen her, Dr. Carstairs had been bested and humiliated by Corona, roped by the neck and led about like a horse. Maga had no doubt Dr. Carstairs would be angry but she hoped much of that anger might be taken out on Corona and not herself.

Maga gulped when she heard a key turn in the door. She felt goosebumps on her arms as the door slowly creaked open and Dr. Carstairs entered. Maga immediately noticed her disheveled appearance and the purple welts around her neck. She also noticed Dr. Carstairs had returned alone.

"D-Dr. Carstairs," Maga stuttered. "The girl...?"

"Escaped," Dr. Carstairs replied in an unusually raspy voice. "Along with the boy and taking one of our Humvees with them." She stepped forward and Maga backed away. "The loss of a Humvee means one less patrol and a chink in our security." Dr. Carstairs reached for her sore neck and massaged her throat. "The girl would have provided several much-needed organs and a few meals but the boy — an unusually virile specimen — would have ensured the survival of Utopia's bloodline. Because of your ineptitude they've both escaped and two of our security detail have been injured. I shall deal with you later. Now, I must make myself presentable and report all of this to Proctor who will undoubtedly be displeased."

"Please, doctor! I'm so sorry. I didn't mean to let her escape. I thought she was dying."

"Obviously, she still had quite a bit of life left in her," Dr. Carstairs said in her hoarse voice. "Which is more than will be said for you. Tomorrow, you'll be sent to the farm and I look forward to seeing you again on my dinner table." She turned and left the room.

The color drained from Maga's face until her countenance had become as pallid as an albino's. She glanced at her shaky hands and realized she was trembling. She knew there would be no reprieve. Dr. Carstairs was not only vindictive but resolute in her decisions. Any appeal on Maga's part would fall on deaf ears. Maga berated herself mercilessly. How could she have failed to lock the door behind her? Such a simple little thing. She looked up. At the door. The unlocked door.

Chapter Eight

Maga hurried down the corridor. A few minutes later, she had reached one of the exits from the domed city of Utopia. There were no guards posted at the exits because no Raiders had ever gotten past the roving patrols to come anywhere close to the dome. She slipped out furtively, nervously gazing behind her back constantly. Maga had no idea where she was going; she only knew what awaited her if she stayed. And that spurred her forward.

Proctor paced about the study, absent-mindedly fondling the devotional medal he wore around his neck, while Dr. Carstairs stood repentantly in place. It was a St. Sebastian medal, honoring the saint known as the protector of potential plague victims. Not that St. Sebastian was one to afford protection to others: he himself had been shot full of arrows and later clubbed to death. Still, Proctor found the cold metal pressing against his chest reassuring in a world gone mad from a deadly pandemic and its aftermath. When his agitation had diminished, he opened a file cabinet and took out a map. He unfurled it and spread the map across his desk. "Which way did the injured patrol you interviewed say the stolen Humvee was headed?"

Dr. Carstairs pointed on the map. "He said they took off in this direction. Even with a full charge, the Humvee can't go past the perimeter."

Proctor frowned. "Sector Fifteen. That would take them within a few miles of the Outpost."

"If it did, they'd still have a long walk and they probably don't know about the Outpost. It's just as likely the Humvee ran out of juice within the perimeter."

Proctor nodded. He called out and a young man rushed into the study. "Donjay, I want all the patrols to cover the entire perimeter, day and night. We must recover the boy... and the girl, too. Have them search every inch and report back to me."

"Yes, sir." Donjay raced out to gather the patrols.

"If they've escaped the perimeter, then we'll have to send a patrol outside," Proctor said.

"But the perimeter marks the circumference of the distance from the dome that a Humvee battery can maintain its charge. The patrols will have to cover that expanse on foot. The vehicles can't travel any farther than the radius."

"You're correct, doctor. Not on a single battery. But if we take a second battery out of one of the Humvees and bring it along as a spare, then we'll double our range."

"Ingenious. Hopefully that won't be necessary. But if the patrols report back that the specimens have indeed escaped beyond the perimeter and are continuing toward the Outpost—"

"As you say, let's hope that's not the case. But should it be, then I'll lead a patrol to the Outpost myself."

Dr. Carstairs gasped. "But that would mean..."

Proctor grimaced. "That boy is essential to the future survival of Utopia. This is too important to leave to anyone else, even Donjay. I'll go, even if it means I'm to confront my past... And the one person I swore never to see again."

Destine and Covid sat with Granny inside her trailer while Archer and Robin did their daily chores outdoors. "I appreciate you taking the time to tell me all about life before the virus," Destine said. "I've never met anyone as old as you before. I've learned more from you than I would have from reading a dozen books."

Granny smiled at her. "You're the inquisitive type, ain't you? Smart gal. You've got some weird names, though."

Covid shrugged. "I guess we're used to them. They don't seem weird to us. I was told my parents named me and my twin sister Corona after the COVID-25 coronavirus because we were born during the lockdown. I guess they thought the virus would pass and our names would mark a brief, distinct period in which we were born. I doubt they realized four years later we'd be taken from them and quarantined in the bunker."

"The bunker?" Granny asked.

Destine shot Covid an admonishing look. "You talk too much."

"That must have been when the second wave — COVID-29 — hit, four years after the first," Granny said. "So who took you from your folks?"

Covid glanced nervously at Destine, worried he had revealed too much.

"You might as well tell her the rest," Destine said. "Granny's been patiently answering all my questions for hours and you've already spilled the beans."

"The scientists," Covid said sheepishly. "They built an enormous underground bunker—"

"A biosphere," Destine interrupted.

"And the government selected fifty infants and children to be future of mankind in case the virus wiped out everyone on Earth. Most of us don't even remember our parents. We were raised by the scientists but they soon got sick, too. Their bodies had to be incinerated in the furnace. Only one adult scientist survived past the first few months and he raised all of us until recently."

"He died," Destine said. "I don't think it was the virus, though."

"It happens, hun," Granny said. "Maybe not to young'uns like you, but at my age you come to expect it."

"My sister decided it was time to see what life was like outside the bunker so she and Kai snuck out. We're going to find them and bring them back home."

"Them's the two you said you was lookin' fer when we first met you." Granny pinched a wad of snuff and placed it up her nose. "I seem to remember the government constructing some hush-hush project about a dozen miles or so southeast of here after the initial outbreak." Granny opened a drawer and took out a tattered map. She unfolded it and pointed to a spot. "This is where we are. As I recall, the government soldiers cordoned off a huge area right about here." She pointed to another spot to the bottom right of the map. "That must be where your bunker is."

Destine gaped. "This shows the whole area we've been walking through! This is incredible. Granny, may we borrow this?"

"You can have it. It's not like I'm going anywhere."

"Thanks," Destine said. "This will be a great help in our search."

"You're welcome. So, this bunker of yours — it's filled with fifty kids your age?"

"Boys and girls from thirteen to nineteen," Destine said.

Granny sniffed a bit more snuff. "Archer and Robin have taken a liking to the two of you. It's only natural since everyone else at the Outpost is about fifty years older than they are. Robin in particular has taken a shine to you, Covid. You probably got your pick of the girls back at your bunker but the only way Robin or Archer's gonna find a mate is to join another outpost; and even then, there's slim pickings. Fifty teenagers in one place! I can't even imagine it. I know they couldn't." Granny leaned in. "I want you to do me a favor: if I can talk them into it, I'd like you to bring them back with you to your bunker after you find your missing companions. Archer and Robin deserve to grow up with their peers; not with a bunch of old fogies."

Covid exchanged glances with Destine. "I don't have any objection — now that they don't want to use us for target practice. But do you think you can persuade them to leave their home?"

"Give me a few days to convince them." Granny pointed to the map. "You'll need some time to plan which way you're headed. You can stay here 'til then."

Destine turned to Covid. "Might as well, at least until we know where we're going."

Covid nodded. "All right, but only for a few days." He worried further delay meant he might never find his sister.

Maga dove under a clump of bushes when she spotted a Humvee out of the corner of her eye. She held her breath as it drew nearer and then passed by her hiding spot without incident. She breathed a deep sigh of relief. She had no plan. She didn't know where she was running to. She only knew what she was running from. Maga's life as a servant to Utopia's leaders had not been enviable but it was nonetheless preferable to ending up as the ultimate recyclable product.

She knew she had to flee Utopia and could never return. But where to go? How distant were the other communities? Even if she could make it to some other community, would they welcome a stranger in a world where people fought over scarce resources? Or would they view her as competition for food... or worse, as food itself?

Maga wondered if, alternatively, she could exist alone in the wilderness. She recoiled at the thought of a lifetime of eternal loneliness. Besides, the wilderness meant snakes, wolves, hyenas, and… Raiders. The prospects terrified her. Maga hid beneath the bushes, waiting for the cover of darkness before venturing farther.

Corona and Kai sat in the stationary Humvee. "At least we put a lot of distance between us and Utopia," Corona said.

"It was fun while it lasted," Kai said. "I always wanted my own sports car but never dreamed I'd actually get to drive a car… even if it was only for a short while." He sighed. " I guess it's back to walking from here."

"Not in the daylight. I've had my fill of heatstroke." She pointed to a grove of trees. "If we can push this over there then we can hide your sports car among the trees."

"All right, I'll push on the driver's side, you push on your side." Slowly, the Humvee rolled toward the grove. Kai wiped the sweat from his face. "You were right; we wouldn't get far with the hot sun bearing down on us and they could easily spot us from a distance in the daylight. We should definitely stay here until dark when it's cool."

Corona nodded. "From now on, we should travel by night, at least until we put enough distance between us and Utopia."

"We won't be able to travel far at night, though. The lack of visibility will slow us down."

Corona looked at her flashlight. "I wish we still had the headlights on your sports car."

"I told you, I don't think it's a sports car. Maybe it's a truck or a train. Destine would probably know what they called it. Sports cars were colorful and sleek in all the photos I've seen. But this was still fun to drive."

Chapter Eight

"Remember where we left the not-a-sports-car so when we eventually return to the bunker we can reclaim it."

"Definitely," Kai said. "*If* we go back. There's still a lot of Earth to explore. It can't all be like Utopia." He saw Corona's melancholy expression. "You're not having second thoughts, are you? Is the great explorer ready to go home?"

Corona shook her head. "When we nearly died in the heat, I realized I hadn't even said goodbye to my brother. If I do die out here, it means I'll never see Covid again. I don't even remember my last words to him."

Kai put his arm around her shoulder. "You'll see him again. We're not going to die out here."

Corona placed her head on his chest and snuggled against him. He gently stroked her hair, gazing out from behind the trees watching for any patrols on the horizon.

Chapter Nine

ARLO AND NICO STRODE THROUGH the bunker in an arrogant, imperious fashion. Nico shoved Tristan out of his path, knocking the younger boy to the floor.

"Hey!" Tristan cried. "What's the idea?"

Nico shrugged. "You saw us coming. You should have gotten out of the way."

Tristan frowned, looking up at the two husky boys. "Or, you could have walked around me."

Nico turned to Arlo. "Did you hear something?"

Arlo shook his head. "Nah."

Nico kicked Tristan in the stomach before the smaller boy could stand up.

"Oww!" Tristan doubled over in pain.

"Still can't hear anything," Arlo said.

Nico savagely kicked Tristan three more times, as the boy curled into a whimpering ball. "I thought I heard something but no one would be talking back to an enforcer, would they?"

Arlo ground his shoe into Tristan's cheek. "Nah, no one would be that stupid." Arlo and Nico continued strolling through the bunker. Fiona raced to Tristan, helping him sit up. "Are you all right?"

Dax joined them, as Tristan nodded. "He just knocked the wind out of me… and my ribs are sore."

Fiona helped Tristan to his feet. "You need to stay clear of those two. They were always bullies but now they have free reign to do as they please."

Dax eyed the two enforcers as they slipped into the classroom that had been unused since their teacher's death. "Someone needs to have a word with them."

Fiona looked at her. "They're dangerous. They think they can do whatever they want."

"Can't they?" Tristan asked. "As long as Varian doesn't stop them, they can."

Dax clenched her jaw. "We'll see about that." She walked toward the classroom.

Inside the classroom, Coralie looked up when she saw the two larger boys enter. "What are you doing here? I came here to be alone."

Arlo approached her. "You always want to be alone. You anti-social or something?"

"She's a loner," Nico said. "She doesn't like people, do you Coralie?"

Arlo drew closer to Coralie. "Maybe she just doesn't like you." He brushed her hair with his fingers. "See, she likes me."

"Go away," Coralie said, turning aside.

Arlo pushed her against the wall and pressed his body against her. "Show Nico how much you like me. Give me a little kiss."

82

Chapter Nine

Coralie felt his hot breath on her face and heard Nico's raucous laughter in the background. She smelled Arlo's body odor and felt his lips touch hers, as his hands glided down her body. "Please, don't," Coralie sobbed.

The classroom door opened and Dax stepped inside. "Let her go, Arlo."

Nico, standing nearer to the door, turned to her and grinned. "Looks like I've got one, too. Now we can both have fun." He came toward her. "Get on your knees, Dax."

As Nico neared her, Dax flung her leg upward, her foot catching Nico in the groin. Nico doubled over in pain, wearing a shocked and anguished expression. Dax grabbed his hair and smashed his head into the wall. Blood trickled from his forehead as he fell to the floor and curled into a fetal position. Dax stepped over his quivering form and gave him a more powerful kick to the groin. "That's for Tristan." Nico's pained caterwauling reverberated throughout the room as Arlo and Coralie watched in astonishment. Dax knelt and whispered to Nico, "I'm on my knees and you're right; this is fun."

Arlo pushed Coralie aside and directed his attention to Dax. "Feisty, aren't you? I never knew you were so frisky." He took a step toward Dax as she rose to her feet. "You've got a bit of wild in you, like we do. That's good, Dax. Real good. I like to play rough, too." He took another step. "I bet you'll be a lot of fun, after I tame you." Arlo took another step toward her.

Dax picked up a student chair by its leg and smashed it against the wall. It shattered, leaving her holding only the splintered wooden leg, which she brandished in Arlo's face. "Maybe. Or maybe I poke you in the eyes and impale your eyeballs on these long, sharp splinters of wood. How rough can you play?"

Arlo gulped, staring at the wooden slivers protruding from the chair leg.

"Touch Coralie again and I'll show you how hard I can really play. Now take your friend and leave."

Arlo sneered at her. "This isn't over. We're enforcers. You can't do this."

Dax stepped closer. "What are you going to do, complain to Varian? You do that. Run right to Varian and tell him his two tough enforcers just got their asses kicked by a pair of girls. The first thing Varian will do is find himself some new enforcers to replace you two losers. So go ahead. Tell him." She stepped closer and scratched his cheek with the splintered chair leg, drawing a thin line of blood. "Or is it over now?"

Arlo gulped. "It's over," he said softly.

Dax leveled the splintered wood at his eye. "Before you go, I think you owe Coralie an apology."

Arlo's eyes focused on the sharp splinters. His lips trembled. "I'm sorry, Coralie."

"You feel it, Arlo? That sense of terror, knowing someone holds the power to do something horrible to your body and you're powerless to prevent it?" Dax inched the stick closer to his eye.

"Please, don't," Arlo whimpered.

"Now you know how Coralie felt." She pulled it back. "Go. And take that slime Nico with you."

Arlo didn't hesitate at the opportunity to get away. He rushed to Nico and lifted him up, placing Nico's arm over his shoulder and carrying him out of the classroom. Coralie was still trembling. Dax hugged her. "It's all right. They won't bother you again."

"Thank you." Coralie embraced her savior. "Why? I thought you didn't like me."

"I like you."

Tears welled up in Coralie's eyes. "I like you, too."

"You're still a loser."

Coralie chuckled. "With a dumb name."

Dax shrugged. "I could get used to it."

Outside, Tristan and Fiona watched Arlo lug his injured companion down the hall. Tristan made sure Arlo saw him grinning as he stepped out of his way.

Fiona noticed Nessa sitting in the social area looking distraught. "What's wrong, Nessa?"

Nessa gazed up with a forlorn look. "I'm hungry. I'm always hungry, lately."

"Then go to the kitchen and…" Fiona saw Nessa shaking her head.

"I've used up my credits. I only have one a day and that doesn't cover my meals."

Fiona frowned. "Here, take mine." She reached into her pocket and handed her several casino chips. "It's not much after Varian deducted his fines but take it and get yourself something to eat."

"What about you?" Nessa asked. "What if you get hungry?"

"I won't. Now off you go." She watched Nessa head to the kitchen.

Keiana approached Fiona. "I overheard you say you were fined."

Fiona nodded. "All of Varian's new fines and taxes don't leave us with much more than the youngest kids."

"I think that may be by design. Varian's trying to subjugate the younger kids while shifting all the power to himself and his older followers. I'll share my credits with you, since I get the same amount as they do."

"I appreciate that. I've been trying to help Nessa and the other young ones but there's only so much I can do."

"Varian's showing his true colors. We have to make everyone else see that."

"How?" Fiona asked.

Keiana's eyes fell on Lucian seated a few feet away. "I think I know a way." She approached him. "How's the songwriting coming along?"

Lucian looked up. "It's not. Writer's block. I can't come up with the lyrics."

Keiana nodded. "Historically, that was quite common among wannabee amateur writers. Of course, the professional writers — the real ones with skill, the masters of their craft — seldom had that problem."

Lucian cocked his head, his interest piqued. "How so?"

"A true writer of songs or stories always has something important to say. Tales and fables have always been used to pass on a message to the masses, to spread the word. From Aesop and Uncle Remus to the lyricists who wrote country music, those writers never had trouble finding the words because they already had something they needed to say."

Lucian's eyes widened as if he were experiencing an epiphany. "Of course! Why didn't I see that before?"

Keiana shrugged modestly. "I *have* read a lot more history and fiction than you. By the way, how's your buddy Tristan?"

"He won't be shooting hoops for a while. He's still sore after the beating he took so he's been resting in his room."

"I heard what those thugs did to him. Poor Tristan. We all thought life with Varian in charge would be an improvement, but even little Nessa is walking around in a state of depression."

"Yeah, things are worse with Varian in charge. You're nineteen: you get seven credits a day. I only get one. And yesterday, Varian started charging me for paper."

"That's awful. It sounds unfair to me. Why would he do that? Unless..."

"Unless what?" Lucian asked.

"History's filled with tales of men who rise to power and become tyrants. The masses must be rallied to overthrow a tyrannical ruler. Rebels used the printing press to spread their message of discontent through pamphlets, newspapers, stories, and... songs." Lucian's eyes lit up. "That's why the tyrants had to silence the truth-tellers — destroy their printing presses or simply take away the paper supply." Lucian's eyes widened. "But try as they might, people always found a way to spread their message to the masses." Keiana left that thought with Lucian as she returned to Fiona's side.

"What were you two talking about?" Fiona asked.

"It wasn't so much a conversation as a little bird tweeting in his ear."

"Huh?"

"Lucian has a special gift and he can use it to stoke the flames of discontent. It won't take people long to see how, in only a few days, Varian's selfish thirst for power is making our lives worse."

Fiona nodded. "Nessa's been terribly depressed. She's lost her sense of self-esteem ever since Varian declared only the older kids could have a say in matters that affect us all. She feels her thoughts and opinions no longer matter."

"Under Varian, they don't. He thinks the younger kids exist only to serve his needs. Varian believes the power he has should be used for his own gratification and not to protect the weaker or powerless among us."

Fiona frowned. "He should never have been chosen as leader. He's becoming more controlling every day. He no longer feels he needs to give reasons for his decisions. But there's nothing we can do."

"Stay positive. Smile more. And sing throughout the day. Lucian has written some fine songs; in fact, I believe he'll soon have a new one that everyone will be singing." A telling smile escaped Keiana's lips.

Tristan knocked on Nessa's door.

"Come in."

He hobbled inside.

"Oh, it's you. I thought you were Fiona. How are you feeling?"

"Sore, but otherwise okay. I was getting bored in my room." He noticed a box of crayons atop some papers on her nightstand. "What's that?"

Nessa reached for the papers and crumpled them up. "Nothing. I was making decorations to celebrate Covid and the others returning but it doesn't matter. They're not coming back."

Tristan shrugged. "Well, they might."

Nessa shook her head. "They're probably all dead. I thought they'd come back and things would be better. But they're not better, are they? They're worse. You're the most cheerful person in the bunker and look what happened to you."

"I'm still cheerful. It's just hard to see with the boot print on my face." Tristan grinned, causing Nessa to smile. "You're pretty when you smile. You should do it more often."

"I haven't had much to smile about lately."

"I know what'll cheer you up. Lucian told me he wrote a new song. Let's grab the guitar from the social area and I'll play it for you while Lucian sings."

Nessa laughed. "You only know how to play four notes."

"That's okay. Lucian sings like a creaky door. But his songs are always good."

Nessa laughed again. "All right. Let's go." A few minutes, later they joined Lucian in the social area.

Tristan held up the guitar. "We're ready to debut your latest masterpiece."

Lucian smirked. "Just don't drown out my lyrics with your pitiful attempt at guitar playing. Better yet, wait until I finish each line before strumming your sour notes."

"I'll save my magnificent string plucking to accent each line." Tristan struck a chord. "So what's this one called?"

The Tyrant King. Lucian beamed. "It has a catchy beat. Listen:

> Of thee I sing,
> O tyrant king
> the boy who sought to soar.
>
> Promises to keep
> made to all the sheep
> lambs led to the slaughterhouse door.

The day will come, O tyrant king
And what a reckoning it shall bring
Your downfall has begun.

You lie, you cheat, you steal
with crooked friends you double-deal
all the while your people suffer.

You misuse your power
causing the people to sour
abusing their trust; making lives tougher.

The day will come, O tyrant king
And what a reckoning it shall bring
Your downfall has begun."

Tristan's jaw dropped. "That's awesome!"

Hearing Lucian's song lifted Nessa's spirits. "Can you teach me to write songs?" she asked enthusiastically.

"Sure. We can start tonight if you want."

"Sing it again," Tristan said. "I want to memorize the lyrics."

Lucian smiled. "Of thee I sing, O tyrant king..." The kids in the social area started gathering around him. By the third rendition they were joining in verse, their young, uneven voices singing:

The day will come, O tyrant king
And what a reckoning it shall bring
Your downfall has begun."

Chapter Ten

IT HAD BEEN TWENTY-FOUR HOURS since Maga had eaten or had anything to drink. Her stomach grumbled and her lips were parched. She had tried to stay out of the sun as much as possible, waiting for nightfall to travel. It was cooler and there was less chance of being seen. But that also meant she had no idea where she was going. She knew as long as it was far from Utopia she had a chance to survive: but not much more than that. Dawn was breaking and she saw a settlement ahead. That meant people and with them the prospect of food and water... and possibly death.

Maga didn't have the strength to journey farther in search of sanctuary. Even if she did, would sanctuary look any different from this settlement? There was no assurance the next settlement would be any friendlier nor any less hostile. The only certainty was it wouldn't be closer. And between here and there — wherever "there" might be — were wolves and snakes and Raiders and God knows what else. No, this was it. It had to be. Maga took a deep breath and approached the settlement.

"Granny!" Robin called out. "There's a woman headed this way. Should I wake the others or just pick her off from here?"

Granny rubbed her eyes and yawned. "It's just one gal?"

"Far as I can see."

"Is she on foot or horseback?"

"Walking. She ain't got no horse."

"Armed?"

"Don't look like it."

"Then, let's find out why an unarmed gal's walking fer miles to come see us. Ain't you got no natural curiosity, girl?"

Archer woke up. "What's going on?"

"Someone's coming down the trail," Robin said.

"Want me to ring the bell?"

"Not yet," Granny said. "Old folks need their sleep more'n you young'uns. No sense in waking up the whole Outpost if'n she ain't a threat."

Covid and Destine, sleeping on the floor of Granny's trailer, stirred. They overheard the conversation and jumped to their feet. "Let's find out what she wants," Covid said, heading to the door. He stepped outside followed by Robin, her bow drawn; Destine; Archer; and Granny. Robin notched an arrow. "That's far enough. What do you want?"

"Water. Food. Sanctuary." Maga dropped to her knees, prepared to meet her fate, whatever it might be.

"Sanctuary from who?" Granny asked.

"The Utopians. If they catch me, they'll kill me."

Granny turned to Robin. "Put your bow down and fetch her a drink of water. I reckon that gal's got a story to tell and she's gonna need to wet her whistle to tell it." Robin went inside the trailer and returned with a pitcher of water. Maga gratefully accepted it and poured the water down her throat and onto her face.

"Thank you," she sputtered.

"You're welcome," Granny said. "Now who are you and what've you done to piss off the Utopians?"

"My name's Maga. I was a servant in one of the great houses. They blame me for allowing their prisoners to escape."

"Raiders from one of the other outposts?" Archer asked.

"No. That's what made these prisoners so special. They were young, like you," Maga said to Archer. "A girl and a boy."

Covid's ears perked up. "It could be Corona and Kai!"

"I think I heard them called that. The girl was friendly and although I only glimpsed the boy once he was handsome."

"It must be them," Covid said.

"We can't be certain," Destine said. "Maga, you said they escaped?"

Maga nodded and took a gulp of water. "I left the girl's door open. She freed the boy and they stole a security vehicle. That was two days ago; as far as I know, the patrols are still searching for them."

Covid's eyes met Destine's. "If it is them, then we have to find them first."

Granny nodded. "Archer, round up enough horses fer them."

"Can we go with them, Granny?" Archer asked.

"Can we, Granny?" Robin chimed in.

"I was hoping you'd ask," Granny said. "Keep 'em from getting themselves killed. Good friends are hard to come by these days; once you find 'em, you gotta stick by 'em."

"I'll get more arrows." Robin darted off.

Granny leaned in to Destine. "You take good care of my grandkids, too — now, and in the future."

Destine nodded. "We'll use your map. Maga can come with us and show us which area to search."

Maga shook her head. "I don't want to go anywhere near Utopia."

"That's understandable," Covid said. "Show us on the map where we should search and you can remain behind with the Raiders."

Maga gulped. "Raiders?" She looked around the collection of dilapidated trailers as the rest of the Raiders emerged curious to learn what the early morning din was about. Maga realized she was in the camp of the dreaded enemy whose raids the Utopians had feared for years and whose captured family and friends her people had harvested for organs or food. "I changed my mind. I'll go with you."

Archer returned with the horses. Robin showed up a moment later carrying four quivers of arrows. She secured a quiver to each of the horses.

"Bring another horse around for Maga," Granny said. "She's going with you."

"I've never been on a horse," Maga said.

"We've never ridden by ourselves either," Destine said. "But we have plenty of travel time to learn how and besides, the horses will do most of the work."

The five young riders waved goodbye to the older Raiders and rode out at a slow gait.

Chapter Ten

Kai and Corona lay on their backs gazing at the stars. "It's so beautiful at night," Corona said. "Think of how many nights like this we missed, staring only at the concrete ceiling of the bunker."

"Are there really millions, or even billions, of stars out there? How big is the sky? It looks like it goes on forever."

"The Earth, too. Everything's so much bigger than we ever imagined. If only the others could see it, too."

"Even this grove of trees is incredible." Kai picked up a fallen leaf and held it at eye level in the moonlight. "As tiny as it is, it's so intricate. And yet, this leaf was part of a living tree that's part of this forest that's sheltering us from the Utopians."

"I think they call it nature. At least, that's what our biology whiz Destine would say. She would explain all that stuff I've forgotten learning about: chlorophyll and carbon dioxide and how it all works. But I don't think she would ever simply lay here and discuss its wonder and beauty."

"Speaking of wonder and beauty, I never thanked you for rescuing me back in Utopia."

"You'd have done the same for me."

"Yeah, but guys are supposed to rescue damsels in distress. At least they did in all the storybooks I read."

Corona grinned. "Girls can rescue guys, too. You've just been reading the wrong books." She stared at the sky. "Do you think it's safer to hide here for another day or to risk heading out on foot?"

"Depends. Once we leave these trees there's a lot of open land. If the Utopians are still searching for us, then they'll see us as we try to cross it. If we stay here, the only way they'll find us is if they decide to search the grove."

"They may have given up searching. We might be able to leave now."

"Assuming they've given up." Kai placed his hand atop hers. "Are you in such a hurry to leave this little paradise?" He leaned in and kissed her.

Corona gazed into his eyes, caressing his cheek. "I'm supposed to be an explorer, remember?" She kissed him back. It was a longer, passionate kiss. "Although, we could always explore right here."

Later that night:

The moon discreetly retired behind a patch of clouds. Corona, lying beside Kai in the darkness, reached out for his hand. She felt its warmth as his palm pulsated in hers. "You're so quiet; are you all right?"

"Just a bit sore from the other day back in Utopia."

"Oh, I'm so sorry! I didn't realize—"

"It's fine."

"I'm so thoughtless. How do you feel?"

Kai grinned. "Like the last man on Earth."

Proctor paced across the study of the mansion in the domed city of Utopia, unconsciously twirling his St. Sebastian medal between his fingers. It had been three days since the prisoners had escaped and all the patrols had reported in with the same response. Proctor could only conclude the escapees had managed to elude them and breach the perimeter. He looked at the map again.

Dr. Carstairs entered the study. "Forgive me, I didn't know you were preoccupied."

Chapter Ten

"I've been perusing the map. The closest settlement in any direction is the Raider outpost in the old mobile home park. They'd have to go quite a few miles farther before reaching the next batch of Raider outposts."

"They said they were lost. If they don't know their way around, then they might have gone to the East or the West instead."

"If that's the case, then they would have found themselves weeks away from any settlements, with no food or water. We have to hope they traveled in the direction of the Outpost if we want to find them alive."

"Are you still determined to lead an expedition there?"

"It's not something I'm looking forward to. But you know better than anyone the results of his medical exam. He's the best potential donor we've ever come across. It's as if he somehow lived his entire life unexposed to the pathogens the rest of us have been forced to accept since the pandemic. You say the girl's test results were similar?"

"Yes, her organs are superior to anything in the general population. I can't explain it. It's a medical anomaly. It's as though they were somehow preserved in amber, untouched by the pandemic or its aftereffects."

"That's why we must recover them, for the good of Utopia. I'll be back by this evening if not sooner."

"Would you like me to accompany you?"

"No, thank you. That won't be necessary. My driver will be armed and I'll have a second Humvee follow us with four men. I'll arrange for each vehicle to have an extra battery installed. That should be a sufficient complement to capture a pair of unarmed children."

"But the Raiders—"

"You forget, Doctor, that particular Raider outpost is composed of a handful of doddering pensioners. My men are armed with rifles; I don't expect any difficulty. My only concern is we may not find the children and that Kai and Corona may be lost to us forever."

Dr. Carstairs arched an eyebrow. "Is that your *only* concern? Isn't that outpost where your—?"

"No offense, Doctor, but my personal life is not open to discussion. Rest assured, I'll do whatever is necessary for the good of Utopia. Any other allegiances I may have had are in the past."

"Of course. I meant no offense myself, sir."

"None taken. Any word on the missing maid?"

Dr. Carstairs shook her head. "Probably eaten by wolves. She had nowhere to go. If the wolves or the Raiders didn't get her, the sunstroke likely finished her off."

Proctor nodded. "Let's hope our specimens have been more fortunate. If not..." He ruminated. "Doctor, do you think there might be others like them?"

"If I hadn't examined them myself, I wouldn't have believed they existed, let alone others. But as they do, I suppose it's possible there may be more of them. What a tremendous acquisition that would be, if there are."

"Hold that thought, Doctor. We shall discuss it upon my return." He strapped on a holstered side pistol. "For the moment, I must be off." He marched out the door, deep in thought.

"Let's stop here and let the horses rest," Archer said, after they had traveled some distance from the Outpost.

Covid dismounted his steed. "I think I've got the hang of this." He glanced at Maga's ashen face and realized the young woman was too terrified to climb down from her horse. "Let me give you a hand," he said, offering to help her.

Chapter Ten

Destine spread out the map Granny had given her. "We must be right about here," She pointed to a spot on the map. "Now, Granny drew this 'X' to mark Utopia's location. If Kai and Corona were fleeing, which way would they head?"

"They'd have a tough hike heading north," Archer said. "It'd mean climbing hills and stepping on plenty of stones. It's hard enough on horseback."

"So, a steep incline and rocky terrain," Destine said. "Not the most inviting route for someone looking to make a quick getaway. Southeast would take them back to the bunker..."

Covid shook his head. "I know my sister: the last thing she'd do is turn tail and come home in defeat. What's over here?" He pointed east on the map.

Robin shook her head. "The river runs south a few miles to the east. They might cross it but the current's strong; it could drown 'em if they tried."

"Then, they're probably nearby," Destine said.

"How did you work that out?" Covid asked.

"The river. Flowing water always seeks the path of least resistance. The terrain must decline as you go south. They'd go where the geography made it easiest to travel. That means south. But not southeast because that's the way they came and it would take them back to the bunker. Not to mention, if they went too far east they'd hit the river. So that leaves—"

"Southwest," Covid said. "The direction we're coming from."

Destined perused the map. "What I don't understand is why we haven't seen any sign of them yet. They left three days ago; it wouldn't take them that long to be well past where we are. We should have seen some evidence they were here: footprints, broken branches, discarded items..."

"Maybe they haven't gotten here yet," Covid said. "We have the luxury of traveling at our own pace. They don't. Maga said the Utopians were sending search patrols to hunt them down. They may have had to stop and hide for hours at a time."

Destine nodded. "I hadn't thought of that. Good thinking, Covid. Now, accounting for that variable, I think we should continue in this direction." She drew a cone on the map.

"What's that?" Covid asked.

"A cone of probability. It starts at a single point, Utopia, and widens the farther out it goes. I've adjusted for terrain and geographic obstacles on the map. I'll assume they'd stay close to the western-most portion of the cone since they don't want to return east to the bunker. So this is the path we'll take."

Covid nodded. "We'll fan out on the horses to cover more territory. If anyone spots them, call out."

Maga grimaced. "What about Raiders?"

"The other Raiders won't trouble us none," Robin said. "What we've gotta watch out fer are the patrols the closer we get to Utopia. They've got rifles."

"What are those?" Covid asked.

"Weapons," Destine replied. "Deadly ones, from what I've read. If they point one at you, move out of the way. Quickly."

Covid nodded. "The horses look rested. Let's get back to the search." The five riders remounted their horses and continued onward.

"It's getting dark," Kai said. "Maybe we should try to move on."

Chapter Ten

Corona hesitated. "It's a good thing we didn't leave earlier. That patrol we spotted was almost on top of us. They'd have seen us for sure if we'd ventured out of the grove."

"I'm sure they're long gone. Besides, their visibility is limited at night. Let's get our stuff from the not-a-sports-car and start walking."

"Wait. I hear something."

Kai frowned. "I do, too. It's getting closer."

Corona turned to Kai, her eyes filled with fear. "The patrol must have doubled back. They've found us!"

Chapter 5

Chapter Eleven

THERE WAS NO PLACE TO run; no time to hide. Corona reached out for Kai's hand and clasped it within hers. Kai stepped in front of her in a futile effort to shield her from the approaching threat. They heard rustling of leaves and branches, heavy footfalls, voices, and an unfamiliar whinnying. And then, the first figure burst through the trees into the grove.

Corona gasped. "Covid!" She raced to her brother and embraced him. "I thought I'd never see you again." As the twins hugged, a second figure entered the clearing. Destine, following Covid, saw Kai and approached him.

"How did you find us?" Kai asked.

"Deductive reasoning, a map, and a heads-up on your escape." Destine gestured to Maga as she slipped between the trees.

Corona turned and recognized the young woman joining them. "Maga! What are you doing here?"

"Dr. Carstairs threatened to send me to the farm for letting you escape so I ran away from Utopia." It was an abbreviated version of the truth, for Maga conveniently left out the fact she had unintentionally enabled Corona's escape.

"She found us at a Raider settlement where we were staying with Archer and Robin," Covid said, as the two Raider teens entered the clearing.

Robin squinted at Covid and Corona, still hugging each other, giving the latter a lingering icy stare. She turned to Covid. "I thought you said you didn't have a girlfriend."

"I don't. This is my sister, Corona."

Robin's facial muscles untensed and morphed into a smile. "Oh. Nice to meet you."

Archer stepped forward and bowed with a wave of his hand. "I'm Archer." Kai reached out to shake his hand, which Archer quickly pulled back. "What are you doing?"

Kai's puzzlement was evident from his expression. "I'm sorry, I didn't mean to offend you. We're not used to meeting strangers but we learned shaking hands was the traditional greeting upon meeting in most cultures."

Archer frowned. "Maybe back in Granny's day, but since the pandemic no one shakes hands. Whenever we meet Raiders from other settlements, people usually bow. We're brought up to avoid touching each other."

"Unless it's someone we know really well," Robin added for Covid's benefit, winking. "Although there's probably not much risk of transmitting the virus these days. But Granny says you never know when it might come back."

Kai gave a sweeping bow imitating the way he had seen Archer bow. Then, he turned to Covid. "Did you see any patrols out there?"

"No, but then we came from the southwest. Utopia's to the north of where we are."

"You'd know if you had come across them," Kai said. "They're hard to miss." He motioned for Covid to follow him to a patch of trees several yards away and pointed at the stolen Humvee. "They drive around in these things."

Corona and Destine joined them. "Boys!" Corona said with an exaggerated sigh. "Is Kai showing off his not-a-sports-car?"

Destine looked at the vehicle. "Sports car? That's a Jeep. No, wait. I think they called them Humvees. It was a military vehicle although some were used by civilians." She tried to recall the book on military history she'd flipped through ages ago in the library. Then, a thought dawned on her. "Granny said she remembered the military working on a project a dozen years ago, probably building the bunker. That means they must have had a base nearby."

"That would explain the military vehicles," Covid said. "The Utopians must have confiscated them after the pandemic subsided."

"And that explains where they got their weapons, as well," Kai said. "We should leave now and get out of the patrols' range while it's dark."

Robin looked up at the position of the moon. "We can be back at the Outpost shortly after dawn."

"The farther we are from the Utopians, the better," Kai said. "Let's go."

"What about me?" Maga asked. "I can't return to Utopia. I'd be killed."

"Come back to the Outpost with us," Covid said. "Or anywhere else you wish to go."

"I can't survive out here on my own; but you can't ask me to set foot in a Raider settlement."

"She's right," Archer said. "The Utopians are our sworn enemies."

"Granny didn't mind," Robin said.

"Who's this Granny you keep talking about?" Corona asked.

Covid smiled. "She's Robin and Archer's grandmother. You'll like her when you meet her. We just need to decide what to do about Maga before we head back."

"Maga saved my life," Corona said. "If she hadn't left the door open for me, Kai and I would still be prisoners in Utopia… or worse." Corona appealed to her brother. "Covid, we owe her our lives. We can't abandon her to the Utopians."

Covid sighed. He was so relieved to have found Corona that he felt as if he, too, owed a debt of gratitude to Maga. The Utopian woman was chagrined, realizing Corona's gratitude was misplaced as she had unintentionally left the door open in her panic. She looked at Covid with pleading eyes while realizing she was undeserving of his compassion. "If Granny and the Raiders won't have her, Maga can come back to the bunker with us," Covid said.

"What about Varian?" Kai asked. "Now that he's in charge, I'm sure he'll have something to say about it."

"Varian will likely attempt to keep all of us from re-entering the bunker," Destine said. "But perhaps we should postpone strategizing how to deal with Varian until we're safely back at the Outpost, far from roving Utopian patrols."

The others nodded. Kai glanced back at the Humvee. "So long, buddy."

"Is it out of power?" Covid asked.

Kai nodded. "We could recharge its battery with the bunker's generators if we could get it there."

Chapter Eleven

"That might prove useful," Covid said. "We'll have to pass this way again when we leave the Outpost to return to the bunker. Maybe we can bring extra horses to tow it."

"That would be awesome," Kai said.

"Corona, hop onto the back of my horse," Covid said. "Kai can ride with Destine."

Corona looked at the horses, examining the strange creatures in awe. Like her brother and Destine, Corona and Kai had never seen a live horse before, and Corona found its size and stature intimidating. "I don't mind walking."

"Don't be silly," Covid said. "You could never keep up with us. Climb on." He reached down to pull her up. Kai climbed behind Destine, carrying Corona's sack. The horses took off into the night.

Earlier that day:

Proctor grumbled, annoyed he had to wait in the hot sun for his men to swap out the batteries in the two Humvees. At least they had reached the perimeter and were now more than halfway to the Outpost. He kept his eyes peeled for roving bands of Raiders. As distasteful as this mission was, he was buoyed on by the prospect of returning to Utopia with the boy who would be the guarantor of his people's future. He didn't see any moral dilemma. As far as he was concerned, Kai was merely a means to an end. Tools like Kai were to be used, not afforded free will. Proctor had learned, or at least come to believe, there were two classes of people in the world: the inconsequential, who were born to serve; and the consequential, who were born to be served. The lives of the consequential — their needs and desires — were paramount, while those of the inconsequential were

107

simply irrelevant. There were those whose lives had value, like the more deserving Utopians; and those with none, like the Raiders, save for their worth as food for their betters. It was a world view he had chosen to accept, much to the despair of his mother and sister. *Like many women, they were weak and sentimental,* Proctor thought. That weakness kept them from ascending to Utopia in the days before the dome was built, even before the pandemic. It had been a different world then, but there were still men and women who set themselves apart, both physically and societally, because they, like Proctor, knew themselves to be better than the others around them. Social distancing was not merely to keep the virus at bay but the undesirables as well.

Proctor looked up, not knowing how long he had been lost in his thoughts. They had arrived. He gazed back at his entourage. There were four men in the second Humvee; he had reserved the backseat of his own Humvee for the captives. Proctor addressed his driver. "Have the men go door to door and round up everyone in the trailers. Shoot any who resist but don't harm the boy." The driver nodded and went off to convey the instructions. Moments later, the men descended on the aluminum trailers like a plague of locusts on African crops, this human plague poised to be as deadly as its viral predecessor.

The elderly Raiders were haled into the open at gunpoint, surprised by the Utopian incursion into their settlement. Granny peered at the man in charge and, on recognizing him, stepped forward. "Proctor! You swore you'd never set foot here again."

"Believe me, I had no intention of ever returning to this plebian squalor." He glanced around the dilapidated trailer park. "I'd ask how you've been, but nothing ever changes, does it Mother?"

"Why are you here?"

"I'm searching for a pair of teenagers. I believe they may have been heading in this direction. They likely would have sought shelter here."

One of Proctor's men stepped out of a trailer. "No sign of them in any of the trailers, sir."

Granny stared at Proctor. "You ain't asked about your sister."

"I ceased to be interested in her activities after she married that progressive do-gooder nearly two decades ago. Why would I inquire about her now?"

"She's dead. Both of 'em. The plague in '29."

"Oh. Unfortunate. Now, getting back to the reason I'm here, it's imperative I locate the boy."

Granny arched an eyebrow. "Only the boy? Why not the girl, too?"

Proctor's eyes widened. "So, they *have* been here. I never mentioned one of them was a girl."

"What do you want with him, Proctor?"

"Somehow he hasn't been exposed to the pathogens that have decreased most males' sperm counts. He's incredibly virile and through him we could repopulate Utopia with the seeds of its next generation."

Granny frowned. "You wanna breed Kai like he was cattle? That's a new low, even fer you."

Proctor sighed impatiently. "I knew you wouldn't understand. Not that it matters. Just tell me where to find him."

"They was here all right. But they left. Gone back to be with their own kind."

Proctor's jaw dropped. "Then, there *are* others! How many exist?"

Granny grinned. "Dozens of teenagers just like Kai and Corona." She chuckled. "You're practically salivating, boy. You must want 'em real bad."

"Of course I do! Why, by combining our superior DNA with their harvested eggs and sperm we could breed a society that grows and survives for a thousand years."

"Same twisted thinking you was attracted to growing up. You ain't changed a bit, Proctor. You think you're the first to want to use eugenics to create a master race that'll last fer some thousand-year reich?"

Proctor shook her. "Where are they? Tell me."

"Same place as the last guy to try that had his dreams end: In a hidden bunker."

"Of course. That explains why they were close enough to make their way to Utopia, yet we never knew of their existence. Do you know its location?"

Granny grinned again. "I know precisely where it is."

"Then, tell me and I'll mount a force to capture all of them."

Granny laughed. "Never. I ain't never gonna tell you that. You're pure evil, boy. When I was pregnant with you, I carried a cancer in my womb fer nine months and gave birth to a malignancy. You decided your own family weren't good enough fer you. You traded us fer your friends in the city who had lots of money but were short on scruples and morals."

"And decades later, I live in an ostentatious mansion while you scrape by in a hovel."

"I've lived a good life building a community, helping others. You've always been a parasite, sucking the lifeblood from others, just like you wanna do with Kai and his friends. Well, I won't let you. I'll never tell you what you want to know."

Chapter Eleven

Enraged, Proctor wrapped his hands around Granny's neck and choked her. "Tell me. Tell me, you old crone! Where is the bunker?"

"Never." Granny coughed and gasped for air. She reached out to push Proctor's hands away and her flailing hand grabbed onto the medal around his neck.

"Where is it? Where's the damn bunker?" He squeezed harder and Granny yanked the medal from his throat before turning limp. Proctor loosened his grasp and she collapsed to the ground. He looked up into the faces of the aged witnesses to his crime and saw the condemnation in their eyes. Proctor turned to his men. "Kill them." They opened fire on the Raiders, who crumpled to the ground in the ensuing hail of bullets. He signaled to return to the Humvees. Proctor cursed his temper, realizing he would never learn the location of the hidden bunker filled with the virile teenagers he needed. He cursed Granny, realizing the old woman had bested him one last time.

Chapter Twelve

FIONA SANG AS SHE TENDED the hydroponic garden
with Coralie. "Of thee I sing, O tyrant king, the
boy who sought to soar..."

"What's that you're singing?" Coralie asked.

"Lucian's latest song. It's quite catchy."

"I suppose if we're doing extra chores under Varian's new
schedule, then we ought to have fun doing them. How does
it go?"

Fiona sang the song for Coralie. "Nessa's been singing it
all the time. It's really lifted her spirits. She's made herself
Lucian's unofficial assistant and he's teaching her how to
write songs. She tells me she wants to grow up to write
songs like him."

"That's funny, considering they're the same age."

"Nessa's always been a bit immature for her age. But I
find that endearing; I almost don't want her to grow up."

"That's your mothering instinct talking. Have you ever
thought about choosing one of the guys and having your
own child?"

Fiona laughed, "Don't be silly."

Coralie frowned. "Why is it silly?"

"I've spent my whole life with everyone in this bunker. We know each other too well to become intimate with one another."

"Oh, I don't think so. We've only seen the sides others have chosen to share with us. People can surprise you, revealing aspects of themselves you never imagined."

Fiona gave Coralie a quizzical look. "That doesn't sound like something you pulled out of a book; it sounds like you're speaking from experience."

Coralie blushed.

Fiona's eyes widened. "I'm right! You're in a relationship, aren't you?"

"Sort of. Early days; we'll see where it goes."

"Coralie, that's fantastic. I always thought of you as a loner. I guess you were right about people having hidden sides. So, tell me about this special someone."

Coralie smiled. "It's someone who makes me feel safe... someone who makes me feel special. We speak honestly, openly. When we're together, I feel like I can open up, and when we talk I know I'll hear the truth, not what someone thinks I want to hear."

"Protection, honesty, openness, communication... it sound like you lucked out. Who is he?"

Coralie glanced down. "It's not exactly a he."

Fiona's eyes widened again.

Coralie looked up at her. "It's Dax."

"Dax?" Fiona frowned. "But she's always so arrogant and aggressive —"

"Not really. Not once you get to know her. In fact, spending time with someone has improved my outlook and

114

made me more cheerful. I'll even sing with you while we work: "Of thee I sing, O tyrant king, the boy who sought to soar…"

Varian and Esme passed a couple of teens humming Lucian's song as they walked through the bunker. "What is that annoying tune?" Varian asked Esme. "I've been hearing people humming it all day."

Esme shrugged. "I don't know. You could ask Blaine — he's supposed to be keeping his ears open to what goes on, isn't he?"

Varian nodded. "Find him and tell him I want to see him." He saw Keiana heading to the library. "I need to have a word with Keiana right now." Esme gave him a peck on the cheek and went off to look for Blaine. Varian entered the library. "I'd have thought you'd have read every book in here by now."

Keiana looked up. "I have. But I enjoy reading, so…" She selected a book from the shelf.

"I need to speak to you."

Keiana smiled. "This should be good. What could we possibly have to talk about?"

"Security. Aside from Destine, you're the most learned person in the bunker. In order to brainstorm with someone, I first need to find someone with a brain."

"What an awkward compliment. How like you, Varian."

"Whatever you may think of me, I am in charge of the bunker now and protecting everyone is my responsibility. It occurs to me we now have four of us wandering about the outside world, assuming they still live."

"Hopefully they do."

"And if the environmental conditions are capable of supporting their lives, then others may live outside as well."

"Quite possibly. It's a large planet, I'm told."

"What if these inhabitants, these plague survivors, are hostile? What if they learn of our existence, and even our location, from any of our four adventuresome friends and show up on our doorstep? Will we be prepared to defend ourselves?"

Keiana's flippant demeanor changed to one of concern. "Our bunker may be a sprawling complex but it's underground and thus effectively hidden. If there are any survivors on the surface, they wouldn't know or suspect we were here."

"Unless someone tells them. Corona, Kai, Covid, or Destine could encounter a survivor and casually mention the existence of a bunker stocked with survival supplies housing only children. It would make us a tempting target."

Keiana came to a realization. "We need to formulate a defense plan."

"You see, we do have something to discuss."

"I'll consider our options and then we can meet again. In the meantime, the titanium hatch should keep any outsiders from getting into the bunker."

"Unless they come with drilling or blasting equipment. We have no idea what sort of technology or access to equipment such survivors might possess. Oh, don't mention this to the others. We wouldn't want to worry the young ones and there's nothing they could do about it, anyway."

"For once, I agree with you, Varian. We'll talk again soon." Before leaving the library, Keiana replaced the book she had selected and chose another one from a lower shelf: *The Art of War* by Sun Tzu.

Chapter Twelve

In the social area, Dax and Ian each held a mug of fruit punch while singing cheerfully along with Tristan, who provided his guitar accompaniment (such as it was):

"You lie, you cheat, you steal
with crooked friends you double-deal
all the while your people suffer.

"You misuse your power
causing the people to sour
abusing their trust; making lives tougher.

"The day will come, O tyrant king
And what a reckoning it shall bring
Your downfall has begun."

Blaine stood a few feet away, listening to the lyrics and slowly absorbing their meaning. "Blaine!" Tristan called out. "Come join us in some song, cheer, and reconstituted punch."

Blaine walked over and poured himself a mug of fruit punch. "What are we singing?"

"My buddy Lucian's new hit, *The Tyrant King*," Tristan said. "You can learn the lyrics in no time."

Blaine joined them, delighted to be included in a group activity. Ten minutes later, Esme stepped into the social area. "Blaine," she called out from the entrance. "Varian's looking for you."

Blaine stood. "Sorry guys, I have to go." He joined Esme as they headed to Varian's room.

Varian, having left Keiana, was also en route to his room. As he passed others he heard them singing various bits of

Lucian's song. He stepped into his room and found Esme and Blaine waiting for him.

"You wanted to see me?" Blaine asked.

"What I want is for you to find out what this damn song is that everyone keeps humming or singing."

"Oh," Blaine said. "You must mean Lucian's new song. It's catching on with everyone."

"You've heard it, then?"

"Just a few minutes ago. It's pretty easy to learn. It's called *The Tyrant King*."

"And what exactly are these lyrics?"

"I don't have it completely memorized yet, but it sort of goes like this:

"Of thee I sing,
O tyrant king
the boy who sought to soar.

"Promises to keep
made to all the sheep
lambs led to the slaughterhouse door.

"The day will come, O tyrant king
And what a reckoning it shall bring
Your downfall has begun.

"You lie, you cheat, you steal
with crooked friends you double-deal
all the while your people suffer.

"You misuse your power
causing the people to sour
abusing their trust; making lives tougher.

"The day will come, O tyrant king
And what a reckoning it shall bring
Your downfall has begun.

118

"I'm pretty sure that's it, unless I missed a verse."

Varian turned livid. "Get me Arlo and Nico. Now!" The forcefulness in his tone sent Blaine scurrying from the room.

"What's wrong?" Esme asked.

"Isn't it obvious? That little troublemaker Lucian is trying to stir up the others against me."

"Varian, it's just a song. Let them have their fun. It's meaningless."

"Songs, slogans, chants... They're more powerful than you think. That's how it begins. They stir up discontent and dissent. What seems like an innocent song soon becomes a rallying cry. I'll have to nip this in the bud." He calmed down and caressed her face. "Go wait for me in your room. I'll join you after I speak to my enforcers." He kissed her and Esme left.

Blaine returned a few moments later with Arlo and Nico. "Thank you, Blaine. You may go." When Blaine had shut the door behind him, Varian addressed the enforcers. "Lucian's damn song is ringing in my ears. I've been hearing people sing it constantly all day. He's trying to undermine my authority and I can't allow that. I want you to teach him a lesson. I don't want him writing any more songs directed at me. Take care of this immediately."

Arlo and Nico nodded and left his room. A frustrated sigh escaped Varian's lips. He hoped this would be the end of the matter yet he knew it was likely only the beginning.

Lucian heard the knock on his door. Nessa was early, he thought. He appreciated her enthusiasm for learning to write songs but he was discovering being her teacher cut into his time for songwriting. Nonetheless, he found he couldn't refuse her innocent requests for lessons and he found the attention flattering. "Come in," he called out.

Arlo and Nico entered his room and closed the door behind them.

"What do *you* want?" Lucian asked as they approached him.

The two larger boys towered over the 13-year-old. "Varian doesn't like your new song." Nico said. Arlo placed his hand over Lucian's mouth. "You've said enough. It's my turn to sing now. My song is *Ten Little Indians*. Arlo grasped Lucian's forefinger. "Here's the first Indian. I'm going to break each one of them until there are none. After that, I don't think you'll be writing any more songs." Lucian struggled to break free but Arlo was too strong. He tried to scream but only a muffled sound escaped Arlo's hand. One by one the sound of finger bones snapping and cracking reverberated through the room along with Lucian's stifled cries. "And that was the last little Indian," Arlo said. "And then there were none."

Lucian had never felt such pain. As much as he struggled, he couldn't free himself from Arlo's grasp. He bit down on the hand covering his mouth.

"Ow," Arlo said. "He's still got some fight left in him."

"I'll fix that," Nico said, slamming his fists into the smaller boy's torso. "Hold him steady. He makes a good punching bag." Arlo kept his hand over Lucian's mouth and held him down while Nico rained blows down on him.

"Okay, he's had enough," Arlo said. "He's stopped struggling." Arlo removed his hand from Lucian's mouth.

"He's not singing now," Nico said, chuckling.

Arlo placed his hand inches from Lucian's mouth and nose. "He's not breathing, either. I think he's dead."

"All I did was punch him."

"Maybe you punctured his lung? See for yourself; he's not breathing." Blood trickled from Lucian's lips. Arlo backed away.

"What do we do now?"

"Let's go, quick." They slipped out of Lucian's room and raced away, leaving the boy lying on the bed.

Nessa knocked on Lucian's door. "Lucian?" She pushed the door open and saw Lucien laying on the bed. "Lucian, it's Nessa. You said you'd teach me about rhyme and meter tonight, remember?" She approached the bed. "Are you too tired tonight? You're not sleeping already, are you?" She tapped his shoulder. "Lucian?" She noticed the blood dripping from his lips and realized she couldn't wake him. Nessa started trembling. She slowly backed away until she reached the doorway. She pivoted and ran to Fiona's room screaming her name.

Chapter Thirteen

FIONA OPENED HER DOOR AND Nessa burst inside, immediately hugging the older girl and sobbing. "Nessa, what's wrong?"

The 13-year old girl simply embraced her, shaking and crying hysterically. "It's Lucian."

Fiona stroked her hair. "Oh. Did he say something that hurt your feelings? You know, artists and other creative individuals can be intense about their work and insensitive to others. I'm sure in the morning he'll—"

"No!" Nessa cried, shaking her head vigorously. "The plague got him. He's dead."

Fiona chuckled. "Don't be ridiculous. The plague can't get inside the bunker. That's the whole point of us being quarantined."

"What about the scientists who died when I was just a baby? They had the plague inside the bunker."

"And they caught it from having been outside. Neither Lucian nor you have been outside lately, have you?"

Nessa calmed down and sniffled. "No, but he's still dead. I saw him. He wasn't moving and he wouldn't wake up. And there was blood."

"Maybe Lucian was playing a trick on you. It sounds like one of Tristan's pranks. I'll look in on him while you stay here in my room, all right?"

Nessa sniffled. "All right. If this is Tristan playing a joke I'm never going to speak to him again."

Fiona stepped outside her room. She saw Coralie and Dax coming out of Dax's room. "Have you seen Tristan?"

"No, why?" Coralie asked.

"I'm furious with him. Poor Nessa's in my room shaking like a leaf, crying her eyes out because of one of his dumb pranks. She's convinced the plague has killed Lucian."

"That's absurd," Dax said.

"Of course it is, but she swears Lucian's dead so I'm going to have a word with those two boys. They don't realize what a sensitive child Nessa is."

"You can't expect maturity from a bunch of thirteen year olds," Dax said.

A worried look appeared on Coralie's face. "Could it be possible? I mean, the hatch was opened for the first time in twelve years. If the germs were in the air outside, couldn't the virus have gotten inside?"

Dax and Fiona exchanged glances.

"We'd better check this out," Dax said. She turned to Coralie. "I doubt the plague could get into the bunker but it's best to put our minds at ease."

The three girls approached Lucian's room. Nessa had left the door open so they were able to peer inside. They saw Lucian on the bed, motionless. "Lucian?" Fiona called out. There was no reply. "Lucian, this isn't funny," she said in a worried tone.

Chapter Thirteen

Dax edged her aside and stepped into the small room. She knelt beside the bed. The blood on his lips and the bed sheet had dried. She saw his gnarled and twisted fingers and lifted his shirt to feel his heartbeat. Dax saw purple bruises and contusions on his torso. She placed her hand on the boy's chest and left it there a little longer than she needed to, hoping she was wrong. She pulled his shirt back down and gently placed the blanket over him, as if tucking him into bed for the night.

Dax returned to the doorway. "It's not the plague."

Fiona steeled herself. "Is he…?"

"He's dead." Dax inhaled a deep breath. "Someone did this to him. Lucian was beaten to death."

Coralie gasped. "Who would do such a horrible thing? And why?"

"I can think of a couple of bullies, can't you?" Dax asked.

"This is beyond bullying," Coralie said. "Arlo and Nico are scum but I can't imagine them killing anyone. No one's ever killed anyone. We need to tell Varian what's happened."

"I can't think of anyone else other than those two cruel and aggressive enough to commit murder," Dax said. "And Arlo and Nico aren't just bullies — they're Varian's enforcers. They do Varian's bidding."

"No," Fiona said. "Varian's bossy but he wouldn't condone killing anyone. Come on, Dax. We've lived our entire lives with Varian. We know what he's like, including his flaws, but murder? What happened to Lucian is horrible but we can't go around accusing people with no proof. We're civilized, not savages."

"Then we get proof," Dax said. She looked back at Lucian. "But first, we have to do something about him."

"We have to tell the others," Fiona said.

125

Dax and Coralie nodded. "Give them the chance to say goodbye," Dax said. "Then, Lucian will take that last trip to the furnace."

The social area was packed. It was the largest open space in the underground complex and had been traditionally used for public gatherings. The 45 teenagers crowded together, whispering among themselves. Fiona addressed them. "Some of you know why I've asked you here. I know rumors have been spreading this morning. Last night... last night, we lost one of us. I'm sorry to have to tell you, Lucian is dead." Nessa, who had been trying to remain composed, broke into tears.

"What?" Tristan exclaimed. "No way! Lucian can't be dead."

"I'm sorry, Tristan," Fiona said. "I know you were his best friend. I would have told you last night but I had to take care of Nessa. She found his body and spent the night with me. There was nothing you could have done, anyway."

Tristan shook his head, "I don't believe it. It can't be true."

"Tell them the rest," Dax said.

"What are you talking about?" Keiana asked.

"Lucian was murdered," Dax said. "He was beaten to death. Someone standing here in the social area killed him."

Keiana turned pale. She shook her head. "Lucian dead? No, that wasn't supposed to happen. I didn't mean for... It's all my fault." Tears streaked down her face as she turned and stared at Varian. "How could you?"

"You can't blame me for Lucian's death," Varian said. "I've only just found out about it like the rest of you."

Chapter Thirteen

"This was your revenge for Lucian's song. I knew you'd be angered but I never expected you to murder him."

"I never even saw Lucian last night. As you may recall, I was with you, and I spent the rest of the night with Esme. Ask her; she's right here."

All eyes turned to Esme.

"Is that true, Esme?" Keiana asked.

Esme hesitated. "It's true. Varian was with me the whole night."

"I don't believe her," Dax said. "She'd say anything to protect him."

"I don't believe Varian's capable of murdering one of us," Fiona said. "Varian's our leader and we need our leader to lead us through this difficult time. The truth will come out but for now we must prepare to say our goodbyes to Lucian. We'll be bringing his body out from his room in an hour and we'll have a procession to the furnace." Fiona took Nessa under her arm and walked the crying girl back to her room.

The teens, especially Tristan, were shocked, stunned, and angry. The crowd thinned out as most of the teenagers returned to their rooms to absorb the grim news and await their chance to see Lucian one last time. Varian walked out, telling Esme and Blaine he needed to be alone. Blaine turned to Esme. "He seems shaken by the news. I'm glad you spoke up. You know Varian better than anyone; you know he's not capable of murder."

Esme shook her head softly. "I told the truth. Varian was with me the whole night. He didn't kill Lucian. But I believe he's capable of killing someone. He'll do whatever he believes he has to."

Blaine gulped. "Last night, he sent me to get Arlo and Nico. You don't think they had something to do with Lucian's death?"

Esme turned away.

"I'm the one who brought them to Varian. If he sent them to kill Lucian—"

"We don't know that."

"If he did, I couldn't bear the guilt."

Esme faced him. She raised her hand to his face, caressing his cheek. "Neither could I. That's what makes us different from Varian. You're a decent guy, Blaine. I don't know why I didn't see it before. Varian can be so strong, so forceful, so charismatic... but deep inside, the same things that make him that way also make him arrogant and selfish, and capable of doing anything in his own self-interest. But you'd never go that far, would you, Blaine? You have limits. You really are a decent person."

He shrugged. "I guess."

Esme looked up at him with needy eyes. "Am I? Am I a decent person or do I deserve a guy like Varian because deep down I'm no better?" She lowered her head in shame.

Blaine lifted her chin. "If you're asking the question, it means you are. I think I made a mistake by helping Varian. I wanted to be part of something and he made me feel like I was, like I was important. But I don't want to be part of what happened to Lucian. I don't want anything to do with Varian from now on."

"Me neither." Esme stared into Blaine's eyes. She placed her hands on his head and pulled him in, kissing him. She drew back, looking at the shocked boy. "I-I'm sorry."

Blaine smiled. "I'm not." He leaned in and kissed her.

Chapter Thirteen

Only a few teens remained inside the social area. Dax turned to Keiana. "What did you mean it's your fault Lucian's dead?"

"It was a mistake to choose Varian as our leader. You've seen the changes he's instituted. I wanted to find a way to show the others he was becoming a tyrant."

Tristan glared at her. "*The Tyrant King*—you manipulated Lucian into writing that song to expose Varian!"

"I was trying to help everyone. I never meant for any harm to come to Lucian. It never occurred to me he could be targeted."

Dax sneered. "I don't suppose in your hubris it would. You think you can impose your will on everyone around you. You're no different from Varian except you act behind the shadows, pulling strings like a puppet master."

"That's not fair. I'll accept my share of the blame but my motives are pure. Maybe Varian didn't personally kill Lucian. Maybe he sent some else to do it. Or maybe someone did it without his knowledge to ingratiate themself to him, thinking they were doing him a favor by removing a critic. All I know is Varian can't be allowed to remain in charge."

"I'm with you on that," Tristan said. "I know how Lucian felt about Varian and I feel the same. I'll do everything I can to take him down."

Dax nodded, thinking of the small boy she had covered with the blanket. "We owe it to Lucian." Coralie grasped her hand and nodded silently.

The brawny Ian spoke up. "He was a good kid. If I'd been there, I'd have protected him. He was such a little guy — it's not fair. I never saw him even throw a punch at anyone. He couldn't have defended himself." Ian clenched his jaw. "Anything you need me to do, just ask."

Corbin, who had been listening, approached them. "If you're plotting to overthrow a tyrant king, I suggest you keep your voices low."

Dax looked up in surprise. "Corbin!"

"No need to panic. I merely want to join your group."

Dax eyed him with suspicion. "Are you going to claim Lucian was a close friend? I told you before, you don't know the meaning of the word."

Corbin shook his head. "I had nothing against Lucian, and I enjoyed his songs. But no, we weren't friends, close or otherwise. But until now, the bunker has been a place of safety in a dangerous world. The thought that any of us — including myself — is at risk of being killed by a murderer living among us is distressing. If Varian was involved in Lucian's death in any way, then removing him may be an act of vengeance for some of you but I view it as an act of self-preservation."

"Let him join us," Tristan said. "I was Lucian's best friend and I say the more the merrier. Let everyone join us if they wish. I'm holding Varian responsible for Lucian's death and I'm going to make him pay for it."

Chapter Fourteen

THEY CARRIED HIM ON HIS blanket — the same blanket Dax had covered him in the night before — and took Lucian from his room to the end of the complex where the furnace awaited. Ian and Dax carried most of the weight; Tristan and Nessa struggled to hold up their ends. Fiona offered to take Nessa's place in the procession but the younger girl insisted this was something she had to do. She marched stoically, determined not to shed any more tears. She was saying goodbye to a friend she had loved, as well as to her innocence, and she knew she would never see either again.

Fiona mourned the loss of Nessa's innocence as much as she did Lucian's passing. She saw the sadness etched on Tristan's face and wondered if the happy-go-lucky boy's eternally cheerful visage would ever return.

Most of the teenagers stood respectfully along the route as the body passed by; a few gathered by the furnace determined to be beside Lucian to the end. They lowered the blanket, setting the body at the foot of the furnace. Varian bowed his head but said nothing. Esme and Blaine stood a few feet away from Varian, looking down in silence. Keiana knelt beside the body and kissed Lucian's cold forehead. "I'm sorry," she whispered. One by one, Lucian's friends paid their respects, saying a few kind words or talking about an experience they had shared with him. When there was nothing more to be said, Tristan stepped forward.

"Lucian was my best friend. There are lots of stories I could share, and even more words I could use to describe what a talented and creative person he was. But the best tribute to Lucian is to listen to his own words. Of all the songs he wrote that we all loved, it's fitting to sing his last one today." Tristan's voice broke, and then he started to sing:

> "Of thee I sing,
> O tyrant king
> the boy who sought to soar."

Nessa, Dax, Ian, and Keiana joined in. Soon the others were singing along, as well.

> "Promises to keep
> made to all the sheep
> lambs led to the slaughterhouse door.
>
> "The day will come, O tyrant king
> And what a reckoning it shall bring
> Your downfall has begun.
>
> "You lie, you cheat, you steal
> with crooked friends you double-deal
> all the while your people suffer.
>
> "You misuse your power
> causing the people to sour
> abusing their trust; making lives tougher.

Chapter Fourteen

"The day will come, O tyrant king
And what a reckoning it shall bring
Your downfall has begun."

Varian grimaced but remained silent while surrounded by the cascade of young voices. Tristan glowered at him as he sang each verse, never taking his eyes off Varian.

Ian opened the iron furnace door. They felt the blast of heat wash over their faces as the bright flames illuminated the room, casting an eerie chiaroscuro of dancing shadows against the walls. Ian and Tristan lifted the blanket and tossed it and the body into the furnace. Ian placed his hand on Tristan's shoulder in a tacit gesture of compassion as they watched the vermillion flames consume the body. Tristan nodded and turned away from the furnace to face the mourners. He wiped away a tear. Nessa rushed to him and embraced him. They found they were able to share their grief without words. It was their second funeral and they were learning how to do death.

The sun had risen 45 minutes ago and the sky was clear and beautiful. As he spurred his horse on, Covid wondered what was happening back home in their absence. Life at the bunker may not have been as interesting as in the outside world but its predictable routine provided a sense of security that was absent in the wilderness where the unexpected was quickly becoming a way of life. He looked up and saw they were approaching the Outpost. He experienced an odd feeling on seeing someplace other than the bunker — the only place he had known for his entire life — and viewing it with a sense of comforting familiarity. He looked forward to seeing Granny again, and to introducing her to his sister. In the bunker, where everyone had grown up together, there was no need for introductions. Meeting new people — the concept was revolutionary to one who had lived his whole life within a closed environment. He tried to picture how the others would react to visits from "the neighbors". Would Tristan entertain them with his jokes? Would Lucian write a new song to welcome them? Covid smiled. They had re-entered the world and found the virus gone; beauty in the sunrises, sunsets, and starry nights; and fellow survivors offering their friendship. He felt good about the future that had seemed so uncertain only days before.

No one came out to greet them as they approached. It was still early morning but Archer and Robin found it odd: someone should have heard the horses and stepped outside. As they drew nearer, they saw bodies sprawled on the ground among the trailers. Archer and Robin jumped from their horses and ran to the bodies. Covid, Corona, Destine, Kai, and Maga dismounted and followed them.

"What happened?" Robin asked, surveying the carnage.

Archer rolled over one of the bodies. "Gunshot wounds."

"Granny!" Robin called out.

Destine's eyes scanned the area. "Stay alert," she said to Covid. "Whoever did this may still be here." She took Archer and Robin's bows from their horses and handed one, along with a quiver of arrows, to Covid. They each notched an arrow and spread out among the trailers.

"Granny!" Robin shouted again. "Where are you? You can come out; it's us." She started toward their trailer.

"Robin!" Archer exclaimed. "Over here." He knelt beside Granny's body.

Robin rushed to his side. "Has she been shot?"

"I don't think so. She ain't bleeding but she ain't moving, neither." He nudged her gently attempting to rouse her. "She's cold, Robin. And stiff."

Chapter Fourteen

The medical books Destine had read described the stiffening of joints and muscles after death as rigor mortis. It had seemed merely an abstract concept, like so many others, when she had learned about it. Now it served as confirmation of the fact it pained her to convey. "She's dead. I'm sorry."

"Dead?" Robin repeated, as she joined her brother kneeling beside Granny's body. "Granny," she spoke to the corpse, vainly hoping her voice would reanimate it. Tears fell from her eyes as she hugged Granny's body. Archer wrapped his arms around his sister, crying with her. The others looked on in sorrow, not knowing what to say until finally realizing there were no words of comfort that could truly provide solace for such a loss.

Covid returned from searching the trailers. "There's no one else here."

Corona walked over to the grieving siblings. "I'm so sorry. Is there anything we can do?"

Archer looked up at her. He glanced at the scattered bodies. "We'll need to dig graves for them before the wolves come. I'll get the shovels." Corona nodded and motioned for the boys to follow him.

"From what Covid said, your grandmother must have been an amazing woman," Corona said.

Robin nodded. "She raised us and kept us safe. We should have done the same fer her."

Corona looked at the bullet-ridden bodies. "If you'd been here, you'd have been shot as well. I don't think she would have wanted that."

Destine joined them. She envied Corona's innate ability to connect with people emotionally; Destine had found it easier to relate to books than humans. Books, she found, were easier to understand than people. One look and you could judge a book by its cover; but not so much with people. "Who do you think did this? Do the Raiders have enemies?"

"When resources become scarce, everyone is an enemy," Robin said. "When the storms come without end; when the heat scorches the earth; when hard times become impossible times, survival makes enemies out of strangers."

"Do you think this was the work of the Utopians?" Corona asked. "They have guns."

Robin shook her head. "The Outpost's too far from Utopia. Their vehicles can't travel this far and the Utopians ain't got no horses. Granny says—" She paused. "Granny said they think riding horses is beneath their dignity. She ain't never had a kind word fer 'em."

"Then, who else—?"

"Could'a been other Raiders. Not from the outposts nearby; we trade with them and they's friendly fer the most part. But there's rogue Raiders we ain't never met before out there. Granny called them the Nomads 'cause they's Raiders that travel from place to place lookin' fer food or supplies. A lot of them have guns. But if it was them, I'm surprised they didn't take the rest of our horses we got corralled."

Destine noticed Maga hanging back a few feet from them. She walked over to her. "You don't feel comfortable around people, either?"

Maga glanced at Robin beside her grandmother's body. "I don't think a Raider would appreciate a Utopian's company right now."

Destine shrugged. "She knows you didn't kill her." She pondered. "It's interesting."

"What?"

"The boys went to get shovels. Apparently the Raiders bury their dead. I've read that was common before the

136

plague. We burn our dead. It's a practice written into our code as a precaution against the spread of the virus. Every culture seems to have developed its own method of disposing of their dead. What do you Utopians do?"

"We live within a self-contained domed city having limited contact with the outside world. Our society places a heavy emphasis on recycling."

"Recycling?"

"If a body's not diseased, then it's wasteful to burn it or stick it in a hole in the ground. The person may have died but the organs can benefit the living. Our doctors perform transplants routinely that save or extend many other lives. Many instruments can be crafted from bones and flesh can be tanned and used like leather. And of course, meat is always a scarce commodity."

Destine gulped. "That's a very logical, if detached, approach. It makes sense in an environment of scarcity but some of my more emotional friends might find it... distasteful."

"I remember being a child before the pandemic. The first wave was only sixteen years ago, yet in many ways it was a lifetime ago. Things were so different. My mother would take me to places where groups of people would gather to consume meals. They served all types of food they made from plants and animals. I liked the ones called hamburgers... and ice cream. It was cold and sweet, and melted in your mouth. But those places are all gone now. Today we're lucky to have anything to eat. When I was a little girl, we ate for pleasure; now, we eat to stay alive."

Destine nodded. "What happened to your mother? Did the plague—?"

"No, she survived although my father didn't. He was one of the leaders of the old city, the one that covered most of this whole area. When Proctor and his followers took over our neighborhood, they walled it off with the dome. They insisted we had to do things differently. My mother was one of those who disagreed."

"Was?"

Maga gazed down. "Proctor doesn't like people who disagree with him. They get sent to the farm to be recycled. The day my mother disappeared he told me he had arranged for me to come live with him and work as a maid. I wasn't very happy but that night he served me hamburgers — the first I'd had since the plague — so that cheered me up a bit. They didn't taste the same as I had remembered them but Proctor said it was just another example of how I had to get used to things being different. He added he had always found my mother distasteful so it was no surprise I did, too."

Covid, Kai, and Archer returned with the shovels. "Corona! Destine!" Covid called out. "Can you bring the bodies here while we dig the graves?"

Destine nodded, grateful for the excuse to leave the conversation. She and Corona helped Robin carry Granny's body to the makeshift cemetery the boys were constructing. Maga watched them lift Granny's body and carry it off. They didn't need anyone else to help and besides, Maga thought, it might be insensitive for a Utopian to intrude on Robin's grief. She noticed the sunlight glinting off a piece of metal where Granny's body had been. She bent and picked it up. Maga gasped at the familiar sight, realizing she was holding the St. Sebastian medal she'd always seen dangling from Proctor's neck.

Chapter Fifteen

ARCHER AND ROBIN STOOD OVER Granny's freshly-dug grave, staring silently at the mound of dirt. The others — Covid, Corona, Kai, Destine, and Maga — waited several yards away. "They're still in shock and bereaved," Destine said.

"Do you think they'll be all right?" Covid asked. "I hate to leave them all alone like this."

"Granny wanted us to take Archer and Robin back with us to the bunker, where they could live among kids their own age," Destine said. "She was going to try to convince them to leave. I don't know if they would have but now they have no reason to stay."

Corona turned to Covid. "You know them. What do you think?"

"I think we should make the offer and let them decide."

"You realize Varian won't like bringing strangers into the bunker?" Kai asked.

Covid grinned. "That's all right; I don't like Varian, do you?"

Kai laughed. "I like him even less now that he's in charge. It's almost worth going back to the bunker just to make his life miserable."

Covid turned to his sister. "What about you? Will you come back with us or do you still plan to see the world?"

"It's a much bigger world than we thought it was and there's a lot to see. I think we need to know what else is out there, if only for our own protection. I want to explore it — but not alone." She glanced at Kai. "I'll go back now and then we can plan a proper exploration expedition — with adequate supplies… and weapons."

"If they join us, Archer and Robin can teach you to shoot arrows," Covid said. "And when you do go, I may go with you."

Corona gave him a surprised look. "I thought you were against us leaving the bunker?"

"That was before I saw what was out here: the good and the bad. We do need to learn about the threats we face. And someone needs to keep you out of trouble."

Archer and Robin approached the group. "We want to thank you fer helping dig the graves," Archer said.

"What are your plans?" Covid asked.

"Gonna find out who done this," Robin said. "And kill them."

Archer nodded. "No matter how long it takes."

"I understand," Destine said. "But if it was these Nomads you told us about or someone else passing through, you may never know who they were."

"We're going back to the bunker," Covid said. "We'd like you to come with us."

"We have food and supplies, and no one has ever attacked us, at least so far," Corona said. "I know you'd make a lot of friends there."

"You could show us how to use those bows," Kai said. "And you could always leave whenever you wanted to."

Robin gave Maga a distrustful stare. "Is she joining you there?"

"Maga saved my life," Corona said. "I owe it to her to save hers. Her own people want to kill her because she helped me. The Utopians are her enemies now, too. You have that in common."

"We all do," Kai said.

"Give us a minute to talk it over," Archer said. He and Robin stepped back toward Granny's grave.

Robin looked down at her grave. "Ain't right to leave her. This is our home."

"She ain't gonna be with us no more, even if we stay. The others neither. It'd be just you and me."

"It'll always be just you and me, wherever we are. We're the only kin we got now."

"True. What would Granny say to do?"

Robin chuckled. "Prob'ly tell us to quit jabbering and pack our stuff before them kids come to their senses and change their minds."

"Yep, that sounds like Granny, fer sure." Archer looked down at the grave and turned back to Robin. "Ready to go?"

Robin nodded. She looked down at Granny's grave. "We're gonna get whoever done this. That's a promise, Granny."

Archer nodded. "A promise."

They turned and joined the group. "We done talked it over," Archer said. "We'd like to come stay fer a spell."

"Go pack your things," Covid said.

"Are you still planning to stop at the grove and pick up my not-a-sports-car?" Kai asked.

141

Covid asked Archer, "Do you have an extra half-dozen horses and some rope?"

"We got a dozen horses in the corral. There's seven of us. If'n one of us rides double, we do."

Covid turned to Kai. "Looks like we're getting you a not-a-sports-car." He grinned. "Provided you teach me how to drive it."

Archer and Robin went into their trailer to pack the few belongings they wanted to bring with them. Maga stared at the St. Sebastian medal in her hand before slipping it into her pocket.

Corbin stepped into the classroom. Varian was seated at a small table waiting for him. "Why did you want to meet here and not in your room?" Corbin asked.

"I'm meeting a few other people today and the bedrooms are too small to conduct meetings with more than one person. They were designed to be quite minimalist with little room for more than a bed and nightstand. And to be perfectly honest, Corbin, I find the thought of you sitting on my bed abhorrent." Corbin winced. "Whereas the classroom is much larger — especially after I moved a couple of desks into the hall — and practically unused lately." Varian ruminated. "Perhaps I should mandate classes, at least for the younger children. They really should be learning. It would give them something constructive to do with their time instead of going around singing songs all day."

"I imagine you're not a music fan after Lucian's funeral."

Varian grew annoyed. "Was there a particular reason you requested this meeting or did you simply wish to antagonize me?"

142

"I'm sorry. My bad. Actually, I'm here to help you. I've come across some information I'm sure you'll find most important."

"Well?" Varian asked impatiently. "What is it?"

"Of course, information this important doesn't come cheap. I was thinking three thousand credits."

Varian laughed. "What could you have to tell me that could possibly be worth that much? Get out of here, Corbin. I have things to do."

Corbin turned and took two steps toward the door. "Now I feel guilty. I should at least give you a heads-up. A group of people are plotting against you. Have a nice day." He took two more steps toward the door.

"Wait!"

Corbin stopped without turning back. "Yes?"

"Who is it? Who's conspiring against me?"

Corbin pivoted. "There's only so much information I can give freely. If you want names, those will come with a price: five thousand credits."

Varian frowned. "You said three thousand credits a moment ago."

"Did I? I don't recall. If I did, you probably should have accepted then. It would've been cheaper than paying six thousand credits."

"You just said five thousand."

"And you didn't agree to that either."

Varian slammed his fist on the table. "All right, I agree. I'll have six thousand credits for you tonight. Now give me the names."

"Keiana. Ian. Dax. And the one most passionate in his animosity toward you, Tristan."

Varian grimaced. "Remarkable. You've actually provided me with something of value. Meet me here tonight after dinner to collect your credits."

Corbin smiled and headed to the door.

"Corbin," Varian called out. "Tell me, how does it feel to betray your friends?"

"Friends?" Corbin cocked his head. "What an archaic concept. It must come from the time before the plague." He continued out the door. He saw Arlo and Nico heading his way. Corbin quickly hid behind the desks Varian had moved into the hall. The two enforcers stepped up to the library doorway.

Varian greeted them curtly. "Come into my new office."

Arlo and Nico stepped inside.

"What happened?" Varian asked.

"What do you mean?" Nico asked.

"Don't play games with me. I'm talking about Lucian."

"You told us to take care of him," Arlo said.

"I told you to teach him a lesson. He can't learn anything if he's dead. Now, I'll ask you one more time: what happened?"

"I broke his fingers to stop him from writing any more songs," Arlo said.

"And?" Varian asked, growing impatient.

"And the brat bit me."

"So you killed him because he bit you?"

"No, of course not. Nico punched him."

Varian turned to Nico. "It must have been one hell of a punch."

Nico's eyes darted about the room, looking everywhere except at Varian. "It might've been more than one."

"He stopped breathing," Arlo said. "Not what we intended but it got him out of your hair."

144

Chapter Fifteen

"You idiots. You've given me an even bigger problem. You've made him a martyr. You saw what happened at the funeral. People are still singing that damn song but now it's to honor his memory. And his best friend Tristan is going to make sure everyone believes I was responsible for Lucian's death until they finally run me out of the bunker. Get out of here. I'm sick of looking at you two."

Arlo and Nico exchanged glances. They left the classroom, closing the door behind them. They stood outside the door in front of the desks Corbin was hiding behind. Corbin had already learned some valuable new information: Varian hadn't ordered them to kill Lucian. And he also now knew the details of Lucian's death. All he had to do was wait until the two enforcers left so he could emerge from his hiding place and determine the best way to profit from what he had discovered.

"He's mad at us," Nico said.

"It's because of the stink Tristan's kicking up," Arlo said. "But that's easy to fix and get back on Varian's good side."

"How?"

"Same as before: We remove the problem. But this time, we do it on purpose. We make a plan and we don't leave a body behind."

"How can we do that?"

"The same way other bodies have left the bunker: the furnace."

"We can't carry a dead body all the way to the furnace. Someone would see us."

"We don't carry anything," Arlo said. "We lure Tristan to the furnace and push him in. One shove and it's over. He disappears and no one will ever know what happened. Maybe they'll think he left the bunker like Corona and Covid. No one gets blamed and Tristan doesn't become a

145

martyr like Lucian. People forget about him, Lucian, and the song and Varian will be happy."

Nico grinned. "When do we do it?"

"Tonight. The sooner we get this over with, the better." They walked away, leaving Corbin to digest what he had overheard. Corbin waited several minutes to make sure the enforcers were far enough away that they wouldn't see him emerge from his hiding place and then he came around from behind the desks. He pondered whom he could bargain with to obtain the maximum return for this new information. Obviously, Tristan would be the most interested but the boy had nothing to offer Corbin. Keiana might well become Varian's successor and having her indebted to him could prove highly beneficial. But Keiana was overly controlling and considered herself too principled to make deals. But, he thought, Dax was another story. Corbin started down the hall when he encountered Esme.

"Corbin, have you seen Varian?" Esme asked.

"In the classroom." Corbin gestured behind him as he rushed to find Dax.

Esme proceeded to the classroom. She opened the door and saw Varian seated at the desk. "I've been looking for you. You weren't in your room."

"Too many people are looking for me today. I needed some space."

"We need to talk about our relationship."

Varian sighed. "Esme, I'm having a really stressful afternoon. I'm not in the mood to pander to your insecurities. Come to my room tonight and we can do the usual relationship stuff then." He looked up and saw the annoyed look on her face. He realized he hadn't phrased that right, so he added, "You're beautiful and yes, I still love you."

"Well, I don't love you, Varian. And you're ugly. Maybe not on the outside, but on the inside where it really counts."

Varian's eyes widened. "Esme, what are you—?"

"I don't want you to touch me after what you did to Lucian. Just the thought makes my skin crawl."

"I didn't do anything to Lucian. I was with you the whole time. You even told everyone that."

"Yeah, you were with me setting up your alibi while your enforcers Arlo and Nico killed that little boy."

"I don't need an alibi. I've done nothing wrong."

"I saw you send for them."

"Yes, but I didn't tell them to murder Lucian. I had no idea the kid was dead until we found out this morning. They were supposed to beat him up, not kill him."

"You think sending two 19-year-old thugs to beat up a 13-year-old boy is all right? You couldn't even do your own dirty work."

Varian grimaced. "No, it's not like it sounds. I just wanted to put him in place. Scare him into line. I sent them because Arlo and Nico look physically intimidating; I don't. I didn't think Lucian would be frightened by me. I thought they'd shove him around, he'd be terrified of what they might do, and he'd drop the whole stupid song business."

"I guess we both know why he'd have good reason to be terrified of Arlo and Nico now, don't we?"

"Esme, if I had known what they were going to do—"

"Yes, Varian? Let me hear you say it. You can't, can you? You were paranoid. You thought Lucian threatened your grip on the one thing you truly care about: power. You thought his song was going to turn everyone against you and they'd choose a new leader. And then, not only would

147

you lose power, but you'd be disgraced and never get it back. You didn't care about me or what we had. You thought you were going to lose what really mattered most to you and you'd have done anything to prevent that."

"No! Not anything." Varian slammed his fist on the table and looked up at Esme. "Yes, I want to be our leader. But only to help everyone. Our lives are at risk every day and I know I'm the only one capable of dealing with the hardships and threats we're going to face." He looked away. "Maybe I did take advantage of my position; maybe I made mistakes. I'm only three years older than you, Esme. I'm still a kid. I make mistakes; my judgment isn't always perfect. Is anyone else's?"

Esme didn't reply.

"Do you really think I'm capable of murdering one of us?"

Esme sighed. "Yes," she said softly.

Varian was visibly shaken by her reply. He cocked his head. "You think I'm that kind of... monster? I'm sorry, Esme. I'm sorry Lucian's dead. I'm sorry I made decisions people think are unfair. I'm sorry I trusted Arlo and Nico. And I'm sorry I've been a jerk to you. But I'm going to change. I'll prove to you I'm not the monster you think I am."

Esme shook her head. "It's too late. I found someone else to be with."

Varian gaped. "What? Who?" he asked, stunned.

"Blaine."

Varian's eyes widened. "That wimp? You called him pathetic. Is this a joke?"

"No. Blaine doesn't have your drive, or your charisma, or your looks. He's needy and insecure and he does come off as pathetic. But he's also kind and decent... and he'll never need to prove to me that he's not a monster." She turned and headed out the door. "See you around the bunker, Varian."

Varian slumped into the chair and placed his face in his hands. He was not having a good day.

Chapter Sixteen

ARLO WAITED IN BLAINE'S ROOM for nearly half an hour before he saw the door push open. He stayed hidden behind the door as Blaine entered and pulled off his shirt over his head. Blaine tossed the shirt onto the bed and took a clean one from the trundle drawer beneath the bed and slipped it on. Arlo shut the door, causing Blaine to jump in surprise and turn around. "What are you doing in my room?" Blaine gulped as Arlo took a step toward him.

"Waiting for you."

"What do you want, Arlo?"

"Not me. Varian. He wants you to deliver a message."

"Tell him I'm not his errand boy anymore."

Arlo looked surprised. He pulled back Blaine's shirt collar and peered down his back. "I don't believe it. You've developed a spine. A real backbone." He released his finger from Blaine's collar. "But you don't want to make me tell Varian you refused a simple thing like delivering a message. That'd make me look bad to Varian. Do you want to get

151

Varian mad at me? That wouldn't be a nice thing to do to a friend like me. We *are* friends, aren't we?" He placed his firm, intimidating grip on Blaine's shoulder.

Blaine gulped. "Sure. Friends."

Arlo smiled. "Varian feels bad about what happened at the furnace this morning with Tristan. He doesn't want any more hard feelings with Tristan. He wants to apologize and beg for his forgiveness. But you know how proud Varian is. He doesn't want anyone to see him grovel. All you have to do is tell Tristan that Varian will be waiting by the furnace in an hour."

"It'll take more than an apology to make up for the loss of his best friend."

"Of course. But it's a good start. From there, Tristan could set any terms he wishes and Varian feels guilty enough to agree so he can cleanse his conscience and ease his guilt. But Tristan can't let anyone know... at least, not yet. This meeting will be humiliating enough for a proud guy like Varian. Who knows? After this meeting, he might even get Varian to confess his sins publicly and step down as leader."

"You think Varian would really do that?"

"Guilt weighing on your conscience can be a powerful force. Just tell Tristan and let him decide." He walked to the door. "I'll let myself out." Arlo stepped into the hall and headed to join Nico at the furnace.

Blaine walked into the social area just as Corbin was leaving. "Hey, Blaine," Corbin said. "I've been looking for Dax. Have you seen her?"

Blaine shook his head. "Not for several hours. Last I saw her, she was with Fiona."

Chapter Sixteen

"Thanks." Corbin headed to Fiona's room. Blaine spotted Tristan sitting by himself, looking depressed. He approached him.

"That was a nice tribute to Lucian this morning."

Tristan looked up. "Thanks. No offense, but I'd really like to be alone."

Blaine nodded. "I understand. We all miss him. It won't be the same without gathering around to hear him singing. I remember when he — hey, I'm sorry. I know you said you wanted to be alone."

"No, it's all right. It helps to know other people miss him too."

"Everyone misses him. Maybe not as much as you, but we all do."

"Thanks."

"Just so you know, I'm not going to have anything to do with Varian anymore. I mean, I agreed to pass on a message to you, but after that I doubt we'll even speak to each other... especially since I'm with Esme now." Blaine saw the surprise register on Tristan's face.

"You and Esme? You stole Varian's girl?" Tristan broke out laughing. "I wish I could have seen his face when he found out." He kept laughing. "That's the first time I've laughed since I heard about Lucian."

"It's good to hear you laugh. It's bad enough we lost our singer; it'd be terrible if we also lost our comedian."

Tristan looked at Blaine.

"We need songs and jokes to get us through the monotony of living in an underground hole. You've both made all our lives more bearable; happier, even."

"I never thought of it that way." Tristan paused. "You said you had a message?"

Blaine nodded. "You really got to Varian this morning at the furnace."

"Yeah, he looked pissed."

"Maybe, but it must have weighed on his conscience all day. The guilt's eating at him. He wants you to forgive him."

"Fat chance of that. I'd sooner spit in his face."

Blaine shrugged. "You could do that too. He's going to be waiting all night at the furnace, where we said goodbye to Lucian. He's desperate to be forgiven by you."

"Tell him to come here to the social area and ask everyone to forgive him."

Blaine shook his head. "You know how proud and cocky Varian is. He'd have to work up to that. Right now he just wants to beg you for forgiveness first. He'll be ashamed enough groveling in front of you in the very spot Lucian's body was honored. You might even be able to make him resign. I mean, if he wants something from you, don't you get to set the terms? Anyway, I just said I'd pass on the message. It's up to you, but don't tell anyone; at least, not until afterward, if you do go."

Tristan nodded. "Thanks. I'll think about it." Tristan wondered if Lucian's spirit might have lingered at the furnace, the last place his earthly remains existed. *Lucian would sure enjoy watching Varian on his knees begging for forgiveness... maybe even singing The Tyrant King. Heck, I'd enjoy seeing that even if Lucian can't,* Tristan thought. A broad smile filled his face. *I don't know if I'll ever be able to forgive Varian, but it would cheer me up to see that.* He stood up and headed to the other end of the bunker where the furnace was.

Archer looked back at the six horses pulling the Humvee behind them. "It's a good thing we been swapping out them horses. Kai's not-a-sports-car sure is heavy. Otherwise them horses would be plumb tuckered out."

"With a dozen horses and a motorized vehicle we'll be able to explore the area surrounding the bunker," Covid said.

"Gonna need to build a corral for the horses first," Robin said. "Archer and I can show you how to do that in the morning but fer tonight we'll have to find somewhere we can tie them."

Corona looked up. "It's getting dark."

"Don't worry, we'll be there soon," Destine said, checking the map.

"We'll have to pound on the hatch and hope someone hears us... and lets us inside," Kai said. "Of course, if Varian's the one who hears us, he may not let us in."

Covid pointed to a spot on the horizon." We'll know soon enough."

Keiana stood in Fiona's cramped room, as Nessa and Fiona huddled on the bed. "A bit crowded with three of us in here," Keiana said, "But I won't stay long. I only popped in to see how Nessa was doing."

"I'm all right, I guess. Fiona's letting me sleep in her room with her for another night. I'm still afraid to go back to my room and sleep alone."

"You had a horrible experience, discovering Lucian like that," Keiana said. "I'm sure you miss him greatly."

155

Nessa nodded. "It's sad."

"You know," Keiana said in a gentle tone, "I think Lucian wrote some of his best songs when he was sad."

"Really?"

Keiana nodded. "A creative outlet like songwriting can be cathartic."

"What's that?" Nessa asked.

"Something that provides an outlet for your grief... and makes the pain go away. And songs can make others happy or sad, too. Lucian was teaching you to write songs, wasn't he? Maybe you should take his place as the bunker's songwriter."

Fiona shot Keiana an admonishing glance. "Keiana, what are you plotting?"

"Not a thing. I simply thought having a pursuit might comfort Nessa, and she's already shown an inclination for it."

Nessa shook her head. "Lucian was special. I can't do what he did. He said it was an innate ability — something he was born to do. I wasn't born with that."

"No," Keiana said softly. "But you do have something even more important that Lucian lacked — inspiration. Let Lucian's death inspire you to create the songs he'll never have the chance to write." Nessa pondered her words. "Lucian filled an important role in our society. Sooner or later, someone will have to assume that role; I can't think of anyone better suited than you." Keiana smiled at Nessa. "Good night Nessa. Fiona." She opened the door and nearly bumped into Corbin as he ran down the hall.

"Have you seen Dax?" Corbin asked.

Keiana shook her head. "Have you looked in her room?"

"It's empty," Corbin said, catching his breath.

"Is it important?" Fiona asked.

"Extremely."

"She might be with Coralie," Fiona said. "You could check her room."

Corbin cocked his head. "Coralie?" He couldn't imagine two more different people having anything in common. "Thanks. I'll try there."

"Be sure to knock first." Fiona said, watching him race down the hall.

"I wonder what that's about?" Keiana said as he scurried off. "Oh well, I should get back to my room. Good night, again." She headed in the opposite direction as Fiona closed her door.

Fifty identical rooms; Corbin tried to recall which was Coralie's. She had seldom ventured out of her room and, to his knowledge, never invited anyone inside. Coralie was practically a hermit so Corbin found the thought of her entertaining a guest odd; especially a guest like Dax. He wondered why no one had ever thought to put nameplates on the doors.

"You lost?" a husky voice asked.

Corbin turned and saw Ian. "In a manner of speaking. I'm looking for Coralie's room."

"Coralie?" Ian displayed a puzzled expression. "Nobody ever looks for Coralie."

"I know, but she must have a room somewhere. Fiona pointed down this hall."

"There," Ian gestured and led Corbin to a door. Corbin knocked. A moment later Coralie, dressed in her nightgown, opened her door.

"Is Dax here?" Corbin asked.

157

"What?" Coralie exclaimed. "That's none of your business."

"Normally, that would be true but I do have business to transact with Dax and—"

A hand reached above Coralie's on the edge of the door and pulled it open further. Dax stuck her head through the gap, peering sternly at Corbin. "I don't have any business with you."

"Consider this an advance on future dealings. Just say 'I owe you' and I'll collect later."

"What are you babbling about, Corbin?" Dax asked.

"I have information to offer you, but it's rather time-sensitive so we really don't have time to dicker. Promise to repay me and it's yours."

"I'm busy, Corbin." Dax started to close the door.

"Arlo and Nico are planning to murder Tristan tonight!" he blurted out.

Dax pushed the door wide open. "What?"

"I overheard them plotting. I figured you'd be interested. I told you we're kindred spirits, Dax. I'm betting one day you'll have something of value to me, and when that day comes if you were already indebted to me—"

"Where and when, Corbin?"

"Anytime now. They're lying in wait — I read that phrase in a mystery novel; quite apropos, given the circumstances."

"Where are they?"

"Ah, yes. Now, you do agree you'll owe me for this information?"

Ian grabbed Corbin by the collar and lifted him off his feet. "Answer Dax's question."

"It's all right, Ian," Dax said. "I understand how this little maggot thinks. Fine, I owe you, Corbin. Now spill."

Chapter Sixteen

Corbin pried Ian's thick fingers from his throat. "The furnace room. Sometime this evening. They plan to incinerate him and let everyone think he disappeared outside the bunker."

Coralie gasped. "Those monsters!"

"Stay here, Coralie." Dax glanced at Ian. "Coming?"

He nodded. "I hope we're not too late." The pair rushed off.

Corbin massaged his neck. "I'll be on my way. Pleasure doing business with you, Dax," he called out after them. Corbin headed down the hall, as Coralie returned to her room, worried about both Tristan and Dax.

Tristan entered the furnace room. He immediately felt tremendous sadness, recalling how he had seen Lucian for the final time that morning in this very spot, having hefted his body into the furnace flames. "Varian!" he called out, his eyes scanning the piles of crates and boxes stacked throughout the room. "Varian, are you here?" Tristan kept remembering Lucian's face, as he lay on the blanket. He realized there were no ghosts, Lucian's or otherwise, there to observe them if Varian did show up. But Varian was nowhere to be seen. *He's probably in his room having a laugh at my expense,* Tristan thought, *having tricked me into coming here and reliving my grief.* Tristan turned to leave but discovered Nico blocking his way.

"I'm afraid Varian couldn't make it," Nico said. "But we'll entertain you."

"We?" Tristan turned back and saw Arlo step from behind a stack of crates.

Arlo carried a roll of duct tape as he approached. "We have an exciting evening planned for you."

159

Nico grabbed Tristan and pushed him against the wall. He pulled Tristan's hands behind his back so Arlo could bind them with the tape.

Tristan felt his heart racing. He knew he couldn't get away. They were bigger, stronger... and blocking the exit. And now his wrists were securely bound behind his back. "Are you going to kill me like you did Lucian?"

Arlo approached the trembling boy and placed a piece of duct tape across his mouth. "No. Not like we killed Lucian. That was a careless accident. Your demise has been carefully planned— Right down to your funeral, which we're going to hold momentarily."

Nico laughed. "We're going to do the funeral part first. It's less messy that way."

"Think of this as an opportunity to join your dear friend Lucian. You'll end up with him, comingled ashes; but first, you'll get to experience everything he went through this morning. Except you'll be alive when we toss you in the furnace."

"Mmmubm!" Tristan's muffled cry filtered through his taped mouth.

"What's that?" Arlo asked. "I think you're asking why we're doing this? Varian was quite upset with us when he found out we'd accidently killed your buddy. He said your performance this morning proved we had turned Lucian into a martyr and you were going to use that to crush him. Varian blames us, but if we tell him you've disappeared that should put us back in his good graces. We may spare him the details though; he seems more squeamish than we thought. What do you think, Nico?"

Nico shrugged. "Tell him we threw him out the hatch. Say he's wandering around outside searching for Covid, ha, ha!"

Chapter Sixteen

Arlo chuckled. "It's been a pleasure chatting; you're such a great listener. But it's time to say goodbye. Off to join your buddy." Arlo turned to Nico. "Would you open the furnace door, Nico? I have my hands full." He dragged Tristan across the room as the bound boy struggled. Nico pulled open the iron furnace door and a gust of hot air blew through the room. The searing flames danced in the furnace, occasionally stretching outside the opened iron door. "Any last words, Tristan? A parting joke, perhaps?"

"Mmmubm!" Tristan cried, twisting his torso and shaking his head.

"Mmmubm!" Arlo repeated. "I'll treasure those last words and think of you whenever I hear them." He chuckled. Tristan kicked him. "Nico, grab his feet and help me carry the little brat to the furnace." Nico latched onto Tristan's ankles while Arlo lifted him placing his hands beneath Tristan's underarms. The pair carried the bound boy until he was parallel to the furnace opening. Tristan felt the heat through his clothes and smoke got in his eyes. He felt himself swinging to and fro as Arlo and Nico swung him back and forth. "On three," Arlo said to Nico. "One."

Tristan felt his body pull away from the heat to cooler air before swinging back toward the flames.

"Two..." He heard Arlo's voice as he swayed away from the prickly heat and then swung back coming even closer to the broiling flames.

Chapter Seventeen

Dax AND IAN BURST INTO the furnace room. Ian charged Arlo and Nico, tackling them and scattering the pile of crates across the room. The pair dropped Tristan, who tumbled to the floor.

"Wait, it's not what it looks like," Arlo cried. "It was just a prank. We were only giving him a scare. See, he's all right."

Tristan gave a muffled response.

Dax grabbed Arlo by the throat and pulled him to his feet. Ian did the same to Nico. "The same type of 'prank' you pulled on Lucian? Fiona wanted proof of my suspicions: I'd say this proves you two are cold-blooded murderers."

"Tristan plays pranks all the time," Arlo said. "We were just playing one on him. We're not murderers."

"And even if we were," Nico said, "what could you do about it? You're not in charge, Dax. Varian is."

"Shut up, Nico," Arlo said.

"No, keep talking Nico," Dax said. "You're right; there's nothing I can do. So tell me, which one of you broke Lucian's fingers?"

"That was Arlo's idea. He snapped them one at a time."

"Shut up, Nico," Arlo cried.

"Like Dax said, only Varian has the power to punish us. It doesn't matter if we tell her." Nico turned to Dax and chuckled. "Arlo did it while singing *Ten Little Indians*. The kid's whole body jerked and he tried to scream with each broken finger."

Dax gritted her teeth and glared at Arlo. "And then Arlo killed him."

Nico shook his head. "Nah, I did that."

"Those bruises I saw on Lucian's body…" Dax began.

"He made a good punching bag." Nico laughed. "Like I said, Dax, we're enforcers. As long as we keep Varian happy, we can do whatever we want. Besides, I never liked that brat anyway."

Ian's fist pummeled Nico like a pile driver. "I liked Lucian. He was just a little kid." Nico collapsed, unconscious. Ian advanced on Arlo.

Dax saw the fear in Arlo's eyes. "Stop him!" Arlo cried.

She shrugged. "I'm not in charge, remember? Ian doesn't have to listen to me; if he did, I'd tell him to break your fingers one by one. Instead, I'm just going to stand here and enjoy watching whatever he does to you."

The muscular youth grabbed Arlo with both hands and lifted him by the neck and leg like a barbell, throwing him against the wall. Arlo slammed into the wall and dropped to the floor, badly shaken. Ian pulled him up by his hair.

"Please, Ian, don't listen to Dax. Don't break my fingers."

"All right. That'd take too long anyway."

Arlo relaxed, giving a relieved sigh.

"I'll just break your jaw, instead."

Arlo's eyes widened. He opened his mouth but before he could protest Ian's enormous fist slammed into his face, again and again until Arlo went limp.

Ian released Arlo's hair and let him fall to the floor. "He was right, though. Varian won't punish them."

"Especially not if Varian ordered them to kill Lucian and Tristan." Dax glanced at Tristan, still gagged and bound lying several feet away on the floor. "Tristan's been through an ordeal; he looks shaken up and he may have been singed by the flames. Why don't you take him back to his room to lie down?" She picked up one of the scattered crates. "I'll clean up here and check in on him later. First I want a word with Varian."

"Mmmubm!" Tristan cried, shaking his head.

Ian nodded. "Gonna need to get a knife to slice this tape off him."

"Don't rip the tape off his mouth; ask Fiona to find some oil from the kitchen to dissolve it. You don't want to rip his lips off with the tape." She turned to Tristan. "Don't worry, Varian won't get away with ordering Lucian's death."

Tristan shook his head vigorously. "Mmmubm!" he cried.

Ian picked Tristan up and cradled him like a baby. "Relax, little guy. I'll carry you to your room." They left, as Dax stacked the crates, remaining behind with the two unconscious killers. Dax grabbed Nico's ankles and slid him across the floor to the base of the furnace. Then she walked to Arlo, slipped her hands beneath his underarms and dragged him over to the furnace beside Nico.

Esme knocked on Varian's door. He was surprised to see her. "Change your mind already?

"Hardly."

165

"Then what are you doing here?"

"For some sick reason, I still care about you enough that I don't want to see you get hurt."

"What are you talking about?"

"I ran into Ian helping Tristan to his room. Arlo and Nico were going to throw him into the furnace."

"What?" Varian's jaw dropped.

"You didn't know?"

"Of course not. Is he all right?"

"I think so. But Ian said you told them to kill him."

"That's absurd! I knew nothing about this."

"I hoped you'd say that. You seem genuinely surprised."

"I am. I'm going to have to do something about those two."

"You need to worry about yourself. Once he knows Tristan's all right, Ian's going to be coming for you… and so will everyone else when he tells them you ordered Tristan and Lucian killed."

"But I didn't!"

"I believe you but a lot of angry people won't. You'd better find somewhere to hide until they calm down."

Varian nodded. Esme turned to leave. "Esme."

She turned back. "What?"

"Thanks. I hope Blaine's smarter than me and realizes how lucky he is."

She gave a half-smile and headed down the hall. Varian stood at the door pondering his options. He was all alone now. He has no friends, no allies. They had all turned on him believing the worst of him. Even those he hadn't alienated by his greed and hubris couldn't forgive the prospect of murdering one of their own. Varian panicked. Fear pushed adrenaline through his bloodstream as he raced from his room in search of a hiding place. It had to be somewhere no one was likely to go, but even in such a sprawling complex there was hardly an inch which the dozens of teenagers didn't visit at some point. *Except,* he thought...

He knew there was one person who seldom visited the bunker's many nooks and crannies because she rarely left her room — and she never had visitors. *Coralie's a loner with no friends and no one else will enter her room, which makes it the perfect hiding place,* he thought. Varian knocked on her door. When Coralie opened it, he pushed his way in. "They're after me. I need to hide."

"Who's after you?"

"Everyone. But this is the last place they'd think to look."

"Why's everyone after you?"

"They blame me for what happened to Lucian and Tristan. They don't understand. But you understand, don't you Coralie? We're both outcasts and we should help each other." Varian was desperate, shaking and sweating.

"Tristan, too? Then, it's true. Arlo and Nico killed him?" *Dax and Ian must have been too late,* she thought. Then it hit her. "What about Dax?"

"Who cares about Dax? I'm the one being hunted."

Coralie backed away and ran to the door. She opened it and screamed, "Dax! Dax!"

"Coralie!" Dax called out from down the hall.

"There he is!" Keiana shouted.

Varian stepped into the hall and saw Dax, Keiana, Ian, and a mob of others heading his way. He bolted, heading into the main area of the bunker. He saw the social area, and beyond it the foreboding exterior hatch leading to the world outside the bunker. He ran to the hatch and turned

167

the hand wheel. His hands gripped the wheel coating it with sweat. If he stayed in the bunker, he would be cornered with nowhere to run; outside, he would be free, with unlimited places to escape to. Yet the virus and other dangers awaited him outside. Varian was conflicted. Then, he heard voices and saw his pursuers descending on him. He pushed open the hatch and clambered out.

Varian was prepared to see anything — except the sight that greeted him. He saw at least a dozen boots and wrapped his arms around the closest one. He looked up and gasped in surprise. "Covid!" He tightened his grip, clutching Covid's leg. "Please! You must protect me from that mad mob."

"You saved us the trouble of knocking," Covid said. "Now, what are you talking about?"

Destine turned to Archer and Robin. "Can you two and Maga tie up all the horses? It sounds like we may be needed inside. We'll leave the hatch open for you."

"Sure," Archer said.

Corona, Kai, and Destine stepped through the hatch into the bunker, followed by Covid and Varian. They were greeted by a wave of shock and joy from their friends. Fiona, Nessa, Tristan, Corbin, Coralie, Blaine, and Esme had joined Keiana, Ian, and Dax in the social area. Many others were exiting their rooms and pouring in to find out what all the commotion was about. Fiona embraced Corona, although Coralie cautioned to stay a safe distance from the returnees in case they had been infected.

"No need to worry about that, Coralie," Kai said. "As far as we can tell, the virus is gone and has been for many years."

"We can go outside safely and begin building structures above ground," Covid said.

"What's it like out there?" Keiana asked.

"It's a vast land, larger than you can imagine," Covid said. "There's incredible beauty and incredible danger. There are also survivors: some good and some evil. There's love and family, hardship and perseverance, and death. And we've only scratched the surface."

"Yet we've made friends." Destine said. "Three of them have come back with us."

A murmur went through the crowd. "Where are they?" Nessa asked.

"Outside securing the horses," Destine said. "They'll join us inside the bunker shortly and then you can all meet them.

Nessa cocked her head. "What are horses?"

Covid laughed. "I think you're going to enjoy the answer to that."

"Not to mention going for a ride in my not-a-sports-car once its battery is recharged," Kai said.

"Your what?" Nessa asked.

"It sounds like you'll all have some interesting stories to share," Keiana said, "but first, we have a pressing matter to attend to." She pointed to Varian.

Covid followed her gesture. "What's this all about?"

"Since everyone's present, we need to determine Varian's fate."

"Don't tell me you're dumping Varian as leader already?"

Keiana's mien turned deadly serious. "Not only has Varian proven unfit to lead us, he has shown he's unfit to be a member of our community. We must decide whether he should be banished from the bunker or if his misdeeds warrant the loss of his life."

"Huh?" Covid exclaimed. "We've been gone a few days and you've all taken leave of your senses? The death penalty

169

is something out of our history books; it would never be condoned in the bunker. We don't kill each other."

"Varian did!" Nessa exclaimed. "He killed Lucian! And he almost killed Tristan!"

Covid, Corona, Kai, and Destine shared a shocked expression. Corona shook her head, her eyes scanning the room for any sign of Lucian. "Lucian's dead?"

Dax stepped forward. "Beaten to death by Varian's enforcers, Arlo and Nico."

"Enforcers?" Destine asked.

"His henchmen," Dax said. "They kidnapped Tristan and were going to throw him into the furnace."

Corona was shocked. "This is unbelievable."

"Obviously, we need to choose a new leader," Destine said. "Since Covid received the second highest vote, I propose he be declared our leader."

"Hold on!" Keiana exclaimed. "I got as many votes as Covid. By that standard, I should be declared the leader."

"We don't need another leader plagued by hubris and poor judgment," Dax said. "Or are you forgetting you also played a role in Lucian's death, manipulating him into writing that song?"

Keiana bowed her head. "That's not fair, Dax. I never meant—"

"The road to hell is paved with good intentions," Dax said. "What you intended is irrelevant; only what happened matters. And what happened is a thirteen-year-old child is dead because you saw him only a pawn in your Machiavellian power play against Varian. I saw a dead little boy lying battered and bruised, in his bed doomed by your machinations, miscalculations, and poor judgment."

Corona stepped forward. "We can hold a new election later but for now we must decide Varian's fate. We need to choose a judge. Since Covid and Keiana got the most second place votes in the election one of them should be the judge, but as Keiana's been accused of poor judgment, the duty should fall to Covid."

Keiana saw the crowd nodding and decided not to push the issue. She didn't care who became the judge: Varian's fate was sealed. He would either be banished or executed. She was more interested in the longer-term question of who would lead the bunker.

"All right, I'll do it," Covid said. "Varian you've been accused of causing Lucian's death and Tristan's attempted death. Are you guilty?"

"No," Varian said.

"Liar!" Keiana exclaimed.

"He's telling the truth," Esme said. "He told me he never ordered Arlo and Nico to kill Lucian and he didn't know Lucian was dead until the morning we all found out. And Varian didn't know they tried to kill Tristan until I told him."

"You're sleeping with him," Kai said. "You'd say anything to save him."

"Possibly," Corbin said, "but Esme's still right. I overheard Arlo and Nico. Varian only sent them to beat up Lucian. They admitted they accidently killed him while beating him up. And I also heard them plotting to kill Tristan: it was obvious they hadn't discussed it with Varian."

Varian sighed in relief. He shot Corbin a thankful smile.

Dax gave Corbin a quizzical look. "What's your angle, Corbin? You never volunteer any information unless you benefit from it. Is Varian paying you for an alibi?"

"Absolutely not. I merely thought it was my civic duty to reveal what I had overheard."

171

"So you're not receiving anything in payment from Varian?" Dax asked disbelievingly.

Corbin fidgeted. "Varian's not giving me anything to say this. However…"

Dax arched an eyebrow. "However?"

Corbin frowned. "He is supposed to give me six thousand credits later tonight — payment for another business transaction unrelated to this matter — and it occurs to me Varian can't pay me if he's been banished or executed."

Dax displayed a self-satisfied look. "So you do have a reason — six thousand reasons — to say anything to save Varian."

Corbin grimaced. "Yes, but what I said is nonetheless true."

Covid looked at Varian. "It seems everyone speaking on your behalf has an ulterior motive."

"I don't," Tristan said. "Arlo told me Lucian's death was an accident. Varian didn't send them to kill him but he did send them to beat him up. And he did send Arlo and Nico to kill me."

"No, Tristan," Varian said. "I swear I never sent them to kill you."

Tristan turned to Blaine. "Tell Covid. Tell him how Varian made you lure me to the furnace room where they were waiting for me."

Blaine turned pale. "Actually, I never spoke to Varian. Nico came to my room and told me to tell you Varian wanted to meet you to apologize. I had no idea it was a trap to kill you. Now that I've had time to think about it, it does seem out of character for Varian to want to apologize. I think Nico wanted me to believe Varian was going to be there to apologize so I could sound convincing to you. He was scamming us both; I don't think Varian knew anything about it."

Covid ruminated. "Arlo and Nico can tell us if they acted on orders to kill Lucian or Tristan."

"You can't believe bullies like them," Blaine said. "They bullied me for years."

"They hurt Tristan even before they kidnapped him," Nessa added.

Coralie spoke up hesitantly. "They tried to attack me, too. They are bullies... and worse."

"Then, they need to be dealt with, as well." Covid gazed around the sea of faces. "Where are they?"

Dax stepped forward bearing a grim countenance. "They're gone... and they won't be back." Her chilling tone precluded further inquiries.

"Good riddance," Coralie said. "I doubt anyone will miss them."

Covid ruminated. "Since Varian didn't order Lucian killed, he doesn't deserve the punishment of death. But he did order Arlo and Nico to attack and beat up Lucian, making him unfit to lead us. He indirectly, albeit unknowingly, caused Lucian's death. The only question is whether we should allow Varian to stay among us or banish him from the bunker." He turned to Varian. "Do you have anything to say in your defense?"

"I never wanted anyone harmed. Not Lucian; not Tristan. I sent Arlo and Nico to frighten Lucian. I knew they were bullies but I didn't realize they were sadists. I was horrified and sickened by what they did. I only wanted to scare Lucian to stop his criticism. Whether you think so or not, I was trying to be the best leader I could and he and others kept attacking me, especially with that damn song. I wanted

173

him to stop the harassment and give me a chance. I never wanted him hurt, let alone killed. I didn't kill him."

Covid nodded. "If he were here, I'd ask Lucian what he thought your fate should be, Varian. Would he accept your explanation? Would he forgive you? I don't know. Obviously we can't ask Lucian. But this decision shouldn't rest with me; it should be up to the one who was closest to Lucian — his best friend, Tristan."

Tristan stepped forward. Varian dropped to his knees before him. "Please don't send me out there," he begged. "I didn't want Lucian harmed. I thought Arlo and Nico would shove him around, scare him, and he'd drop the whole stupid song stuff. I wanted to be a good leader, to help everyone. But I made mistakes, I took advantage of my position. Lucian realized that before I did and tried to tell everyone. I should have listened to his words, seen what he thought I was becoming. But that's not me, not really. I'm not a tyrant. I'm not a monster. I'm just a kid who wasn't mature enough for the responsibility I assumed. That, and my poor judgment, cost Lucian his life and that'll be on my conscience forever. I'm sorry I trusted Arlo and Nico. I'm sorry Lucian's dead. I'd do anything to undo it if I could, Tristan. But the bunker has been my home all my life; these people are the only family I've ever known." He looked at the hatch. "Out there... I have nothing."

Tristan had stood impassively, giving Varian a hardened stare the whole time he was speaking. Varian gazed up at him with pleading eyes, realizing Tristan blamed him for his best friend's death. Tristan took a step closer and spit in his face. He turned his back to Varian, as the spittle dripped down his face. Varian realized he wouldn't be able to persuade Tristan to forgive him. "Tristan. I deserved that. I don't blame you for banishing me. I'd probably have done the same in your place." He paused, and added softly, "I know you won't believe me now — maybe one day — but I am truly sorry they killed Lucian."

Destine offered Varian her canteen. "Drink it sparingly. It gets hot out there."

Covid and Kai each slipped an arm beneath Varian's underarms and lifted him to his feet. "Corona, open the hatch," Covid said.

His back still turned to Varian, Tristan said in a forceful monotone: "Let him stay." Tristan's laconic words delivered in an unexpressive tone stunned everyone in the social area, especially Varian. Covid and Kai released him, as he fell back to his knees. Emotionally spent, Varian crawled toward Tristan, and looked up at him. "Why?"

Tristan, facing Nessa and Fiona, still didn't turn back. "Because I'm not you, Varian." He looked at Nessa and Fiona, who gave him an approving smile, and walked out.

Chapter Eighteen

A Week Later:

TRISTAN LOOKED UP WHEN HE heard the knock on his door. "Come in."

Nessa stepped inside. "I'm not disturbing you, am I?"

Tristan shook his head. "I've just been lying in bed thinking."

Nessa climbed onto the bed and sat at its foot. "What about?"

"All the changes this past week. It's weird having strangers in the bunker."

"Don't you like Archer and Robin? They seem nice. Maga doesn't talk to me, though."

"I spent a little time with Archer; he showed me how to shoot an arrow. Next week he'll have to show me how to hit something with it." They both laughed. "You're pretty when you laugh."

"You told me that before."

"It's still true."

"You always make me laugh."

Tristan grinned. "That's my job: I'm the bunker's jester — the clown, the funnyman, the prankster, the comedian. But these days, since Lucian died, I've been the sad clown. What you do when you lose your best friend?"

Nessa shrugged. "I guess you let someone else be your best friend." She edged closer. "Can I be your new best friend?"

Tristan wiped away a tear and nodded. Nessa snuggled up beside him and placed her head on his chest. "I miss him, too."

Varian paused as he was passing the infirmary. He poked his head in when he noticed Fiona rifling through a cabinet. He stepped inside. "Is someone sick?"

"No. One of the younger kids cut himself. I know we have some adhesive bandage strips in here somewhere."

Varian looked from left to right. "Where is he?"

"It wasn't serious enough to bring him to the infirmary. He doesn't really need the bandage: the younger kids wear it as a badge of honor."

"Varian the tyrant king would have called that wasteful. Whereas you realize a bandage can serve an emotional need as well as a physical one. You've always been one of our most compassionate souls, Fiona."

Fiona blushed. "Maybe I just see people differently. Little boys try to put on a brave face but their cuts and bruises hurt the same as girls' do. They think not showing pain makes them appear strong but I know deep down they need a hug and a sympathetic ear."

Chapter Eighteen

"When Lucian's death was announced, you were the only one who defended me. And you did it again when they were all ready to banish me."

"I know you, Varian. Maybe better than you know yourself." She shook her head. "You're not a murderer. You have weaknesses and moral failings but you can learn to overcome them."

"I wish everyone else felt that way. They look at me like I'm an inhuman monster."

"They heard you accused of sending your enforcers to beat up Lucian; they put themselves in his place and imagined it could have been them."

"I never wanted Lucian harmed; the idea was to scare him."

"I know, but instead you scared everyone else. They don't trust you anymore. You'll have to regain their trust. It's going to take a lot of work. And time. Eventually, people will realize the real villains were Nico and Arlo."

"Still, I must share some of the blame. I shouldn't have even had enforcers, let alone sicced them on Lucian." He shook his head. "Putting guys like Arlo and Nico in a position of authority... What was I thinking?"

"You'll make a fine leader one day — when you've had sufficient time to acquire the necessary maturity and judgment. You're not a bad person, Varian; but you could be so much better."

Varian chuckled. "No one will ever trust me to be leader again." He turned serious. "I know I'll never be in charge; that's not what I want anymore. I'd settle for..." His voice trailed off.

"For what?"

"Whenever I see Nessa and Tristan I can't bear to look at their faces. To see such hatred, and to know I deserve it..."

"They don't hate you. I talk to Nessa all the time. I've told her you never meant Lucian any harm."

"Maybe, but I know Tristan hates me. He despises me."

"It'll take a lot of work to earn his friendship but he's a fair person. When he realized you weren't behind Lucian's death or the attempt on his own life he kept you from being banished."

Varian nodded. "He showed me mercy but not forgiveness. Given my hubris, would I have done the same?"

"He set a standard to which you may aspire. You can be just as fair, as noble, as compassionate if you try, Varian. I have faith in you."

Varian looked into her eyes. "You always have, haven't you Fiona?"

She smiled at him.

"Now that we can leave the bunker, a lot of people like to sit outside and watch the stars at night. If you don't have plans this evening, would you like to join me outside?"

She gave him another smile. "That sounds lovely."

Esme walked hand-in-hand with Blaine outside the bunker, staring up at the newly constructed watchtower. "Did you build that whole thing?"

"I tied the logs together. And I mixed the paste we used to glue them together. But Ian lifted the logs and carried them here, and Kai and Covid did most of the actual building. You should see the job they did helping Archer and Robin build the corral for the horses."

She squeezed his hand. "Your job on the watchtower's quite impressive."

"It's part of our new security initiative. Now that we're building an aboveground camp we need to protect it and keep guard for threats."

180

Chapter Eighteen

"You mean the Nomads, Raiders, and Utopians? I get them confused. Besides, Archer and Robin are Raiders and they seem friendly, and Maga's a Utopian and she doesn't seem threatening."

"Maybe not, but I've noticed Kai's body language whenever the subject of the Utopians comes up. He always seems uneasy and subconsciously covers his crotch."

"Maybe I should try to get to know Maga better," Esme said. "After all, she's sort of one of us now, right?"

A few yards away, Kai and Corona were standing beside the Humvee. "All I'm asking is for you to talk to Covid. You're his sister; he'll listen to you."

"It's not that simple," Corona said. "He respects Destine's opinion. Covid views her as almost a mentor."

"That may be, but she's totally wrong about the battery. I need to hook it up to our generators to recharge it so I can repower the not-a-sports-car. Otherwise, it's just going to sit here like a dead weight."

"Technically, no one's in charge so you don't need anyone's permission but if you did hook it up and it blew out our generators like she fears it could, we'd all be in huge trouble."

"I know, but that won't happen. I'm the last one to care about breaking the rules but if Covid can convince Destine it's safe, then I can get the not-a-sports-car up and running without looking like a menace to the community."

Corona grinned. "I know how much you want your toy back. I'll talk to him at dinner."

"You're the best." Kai leaned in and kissed her.

Varian knocked on Keiana's door. "I got your message."

"Come in."

181

Varian closed the door behind him. "Why did you send for me?"

"To continue our conversation. Frankly, I wasn't about to shed a tear if you had been banished or worse, but since you're still here you can play a vital role in the project you first proposed to me: protecting the bunker from outside forces."

Varian took a deep breath. "I had surmised there might be threats emanating from any potential survivors. From what Kai and Covid report, it would appear my fears were justified."

Keiana nodded. "Unfortunately. Until we can select a new leader we'll have to work together in the spirit of cooperation, if only to ensure our survival."

Varian shot her a sly glance. "You're afraid they'll end up choosing Covid, aren't you?"

"Thanks to you, my reputation's been soiled by Lucian's murder as well. Be that as it may, there are more pressing matters to concern us. Corona and Kai didn't share their entire ordeal with the others. Some of the details were too grisly and disturbing for the younger children to hear. While the Raiders may come for our supplies, the greatest threat is posed by the Utopians."

"How so? Because of their advanced technology?"

"In part, but more disturbingly they don't view outsiders as equals, or even as human beings. They use the Raiders they capture as unwilling organ donors and process their remains as food."

Varian gaped. "They're cannibals!"

"Not like the jungle natives stirring stew pots in our picture books. According to Corona, they have a modern processing plant they call the farm where people are recycled outside their domed city and returned as packaged portions of meat."

"Then, they not only will want our supplies but they'll view us as a source of human organs and food, both essential to their survival!"

"It's worse than that," Keiana said. "According to Kai, they developed a vaccine against the virus but it had the unintended consequence of rendering Utopia's male population infertile. The Raiders were never given their vaccine, but the virus left behind pathogens in the environment that significantly decreased all the other male survivors' sperm counts. However, they tested Kai and found him to be the most virile male they had ever encountered. None of us was exposed to the pathogens over the past twelve years. Kai says they want to drain our sperm and collect our eggs before they harvest our organs and send us to their farm. You can see why we didn't share any of this with the younger children."

Varian gasped. "It's enough to give any of us nightmares. At least they don't know where we are, do they?"

Keiana shook her head. "Kai and Corona told them they were lost. But they know we exist, they want what we have, and sooner or later they'll find us. We have to be prepared for that day."

"I saw the watchtower go up and I know Robin and Archer have been teaching everyone how to make and shoot bows and arrows. What else is being done to fortify the bunker's defenses?"

"That's why you're here. You were the one who first brought the potential threat to my attention. I assume you must have had some ideas. I want you to work with us to protect the bunker."

"You trust me?"

"I trust you want to stay alive and not end up in the hands of the Utopians. And I know you have the necessary leadership qualities to keep us alive as you always claimed. It galls me to say this, Varian, but we need you. Not as our leader but as an integral member of an elite team working to save the bunker. Are you in?"

Varian nodded. "Of course. You can count on me."

Keiana grimaced. "I hope so." She felt as though she were recruiting a viper to protect her from a pack of wolves.

Covid saw Varian leaving Keiana's room. He knocked on her door. "I just saw Varian; what did he want?"

"He's a conniver and a strategist; we could use his talents. What can I do for you?"

"Come with me to see Destine. Corona wants me to convince her to let Kai hook up his vehicle's battery to our generators to recharge it. Destine thinks it could short out all of our power."

"Destine's rather smart. I doubt it's likely, but why take the risk?"

"Destine and I found a storehouse of food and other supplies near the Outpost. It had been claimed by Robin and Archer's band of Raiders and the other Raiders steered clear of it. When they discover everyone at the Outpost has been slaughtered, my guess is they'll raid the storehouse and clean it out."

"Unless we get there first. But we only have a dozen horses and we won't be able to carry much back to the bunker. It would require many trips and exposing the riders to the risk of being shot, either by Raider arrows or Utopian bullets."

Chapter Eighteen

"However, we could fit a lot inside the not-a-sports-car and only the driver would be at risk. Archer says their arrows bounce off those vehicles and bullets might, too."

"And Kai would be willing to assume the risk?"

"Kai's always been reckless and impulsive. He'd volunteer in a second — especially if it meant getting to drive his not-a-sports-car."

"So if we present it that way to Destine, you think she'll change her mind about charging the battery?"

"Absolutely. She was in the storehouse with me; she knows what it contains. Of course, I'll have to get Archer and Robin's permission to bring their supplies here but I can't see how they would object when the alternative is leaving them for other Raiders to steal."

Keiana nodded. "After you talk with them, come get me and we'll see Destine together. This could alleviate the food shortage Varian feared until the outdoor gardens we're planting bloom and help us lay in a food supply in the event of a siege."

Covid found Robin and Archer outside the bunker planting seeds in the garden and joined them. "I wanted to thank you again for sharing your seeds with us. I know everyone is looking forward to eating the new fruits and vegetables that grow from them."

"We're happy to share them," Archer said. "There's more seeds at the Outpost than Robin and I could ever harvest even if we was still living there."

"I know it must have been painful for you to return to get them."

"Nah, we done lived there our whole lives," Archer said. "It's still home, 'cepting without Granny and the others."

"I wanted to ask another favor of you two."

"Anything," Robin said, smiling at Covid.

"Let's hear him out first and see what he wants," Archer said.

Robin shot her brother a displeased look but realized he was right. "What is it you want?" she asked Covid.

"Your cache of supplies in your store where we first met you. When the other Raiders learn your outpost has been destroyed and everyone else killed, I suspect they'll come for it. I propose we bring as much as we can to the bunker where it will be safe."

"So you're saying we should let you eat all of our food instead of other Raiders?" Archer asked.

"If you have other Raider friends you want to share it with, that's your business. But from what you've told me about Raiders they take whatever they can."

"Archer, you know he's right," Robin said. "As soon as the other outposts learn what happened they'll raid our store and there won't even be crumbs left. These folks done shared their food with us and gave us shelter. They even helped bury our dead. Let 'em take whatever they want."

Archer nodded. "All right. I'll ride back to the Outpost and get enough saddlebags fer all the horses."

"That won't be necessary," Covid said. "I'm hoping we can use Kai's vehicle to transport the supplies." He braced himself for his meeting with Destine.

Kai grinned as he hooked up the Humvee battery to the bunker's generators.

"How long do you think it will take to give it a full charge?" Covid asked.

Kai shrugged. "I'll leave it hooked up overnight just to be certain. Then I can start out for the store in the morning."

"Are you sure you'll be able to find it? Destine or I could come with you."

"If you do, that leaves less room in the not-a-sports-car for supplies. Don't worry; I'll have the map with me and you've marked the spot."

"Be careful when you go," Corona said in a worried tone.

Kai smiled. "This is the sort of thing I live for. I'll leave in the morning and be back by late afternoon."

Corona returned his smile with a heavy sigh.

Kai was up at dawn, eager to get back behind the wheel of his not-a-sports-car. He sat inside the Humvee and flipped the lever. He smiled as the engine turned over. A cheer went up from the crowd that had gathered outside and Kai waved goodbye as he set off.

In his office in Utopia, Proctor reached for his neck and then lowered his hand in frustration. Dr. Carstairs noticed his agitation and asked if anything was wrong. "I must have lost my St. Sebastian medal."

"Perhaps you lost it on your excursion to the Outpost. You never told me what transpired there. Was your mother—?"

"I told you the mission was a failure. The children weren't there. They've gone back to wherever they came from and we'll never see them again. That's all you need to know."

"Of course, sir. I didn't mean to pry. Would you like me to bring you some anxiety pills?"

"Doctor, I—" Proctor was interrupted by a young man bursting into the room.

"Donjay, you know better than to barge into my office, especially when I'm conferring with someone."

"I'm sorry, sir, but I thought you'd want to know immediately."

"Know what?" Proctor's eyes narrowed. "What fresh hell has this morning brought?"

"The stolen Humvee," Donjay said. "It must've been fully powered up: the tracking signal's coming in loud and clear."

"The Humvee Kai and Corona escaped in?" Dr. Carstairs asked. "But the tracker wasn't working."

"It won't work if the charge drops below fifty percent," Donjay said. "Someone must have given it a full charge."

Proctor's eyes lit up. "Either they found an unused working generator on their travels, which is unlikely, or they used the generator powering their bunker. What are the coordinates?"

Donjay handed him a slip of paper. Proctor pulled out his map and a ruler. He drew two perpendicular lines and pointed to their intersection. "That's where the Humvee was charged. And most likely, the location of their hidden bunker." A Cheshire grin enveloped Proctor's face. "We have them, Dr. Carstairs. Not simply Kai and Corona but all of them!"

Chapter Nineteen

MAGA SAT ALONE IN THE social area perusing the St. Sebastian medal. Now that the surface was open to them, most of the teenagers preferred to spend their time outdoors basking in the sunlight, even competing for the new phenomenon of sporting a suntan. There was plenty of work to be done outside including building structures that would form a future base camp above the bunker. Fortunately, the library had several books on building and carpentry and one of the storerooms and had been presciently stocked with an array of hand tools. Still, Maga found it ironic to be the only person occupying what she had been told was the social area. Yet the solitude did give her time to think. She stared at the St. Sebastian medal. There could be no doubt about it: it was definitely Proctor's. The man had been an ever-present figure looming over her life ever since the initial days of the pandemic when he had led a small band in revolt against the governing powers of their city. It was Proctor who had killed her father and taken her mother. It was

Proctor who had separated her from her toddler brother. It was Proctor who had turned her from a spoiled child of a wealthy political family into his maid. It was Proctor's medallion for she had seen it dangling from his neck the entire time. And if it was lying beside Granny's body at the Outpost, it could only mean one thing: Proctor had committed the massacre.

Maga tried to picture the scene. There must have been a struggle during which Granny ripped the St. Sebastian medal from Proctor's neck. It all led to one inescapable conclusion: her people were responsible for slaughtering the Raiders at the Outpost and killing Archer and Robin's grandmother. If she felt like a pariah now, how would Maga feel when they learned the truth?

"You look so deep in thought."

Maga looked up at the girl who had entered the social area.

"I'm Esme. I know it must be hard to keep track of all the names. I've had my whole life to learn everyone's names and you've only had a week."

"Yes," Maga said uneasily.

Esme noticed the medal in her hands. "What's that?"

Maga quickly slipped it into her pocket. "Nothing."

"You'll like it here. The bunker's a friendly place."

"That boy Tristan doesn't seem to like me. He gives me odd looks whenever we pass in the halls. Have I done something to offend him?"

"No, Tristan's usually friendly and cheerful. His best friend died recently and he hasn't been himself."

"Maybe I'm being too sensitive but even this morning he glowered at me as I came out of the bedroom."

"Oh," Esme said. "The bunker was built to house fifty of us. When you and Archer and Robin came to stay with us,

Chapter Nineteen

Archer and Robin were given Arlo and Nico's rooms and you were given Lucian's room. I guess Tristan finds it unsettling to see anyone other than Lucian coming out of his best friend's room."

"So I'm sleeping in the same bed someone was murdered in?"

"Oh, they washed the sheets." Esme paused. "It's usually not like this in the bunker. We've never had a murder before. If you're uncomfortable staying in that room, there are the grown-ups' quarters. The only one using them also died several weeks ago and nobody's been in since. You could pass for much older anyway. How old are you?"

"Twenty-three."

"Wow. So you remember what it was like before the plague."

"Only bits and pieces. My brother and I were young children when the first wave hit. I was seven and he was four. I don't remember anything before then. The plague killed a lot of people and then it went away. We were able to leave our homes and go places. We played with other children. I remember school and the playground and places we would go to eat or shop. And then, four years later, it came back. We were locked up in our houses again but that didn't keep everyone safe this time. So many people died in the second wave. My father said at least eighty percent of the population. It was nothing like the first time."

Esme sat listening spellbound, hanging on every word.

"Finally, it ended. People stopped getting sick and dying. I was eleven years old and I tried to comfort my little eight-year-old brother like any good big sister would. I told him the worst was over and everything was going to be all right now." Maga closed her eyes and shook her head. " I was so wrong."

"Why? What happened?" Esme asked.

"Politics. Back then, the world had been filled with people divided into countries. We had a photograph of our country's leader on the wall of our home. My parents worshiped him and believed him when he said he would bring greatness to our country. They even named my brother and me after him. He brought many changes but when all the governments fell and every local community had to become its own nation, Proctor and his friends emerged from their homes with guns and automatic weapons. Proctor said the great leader, despite all his drastic changes, hadn't gone far enough. Proctor took charge of what remained of our city and killed everyone who stood in his way, including my father. He moved everyone that was left, only about eight hundred survivors, into the nicest neighborhood and walled us in with a huge dome. They called it Utopia."

"What sort of place is Utopia?"

"It depends on who you are. Proctor's a misogynist: he thinks girls like us have little value other than to serve men. That's why he took me in and made me a maid and had me look after my brother until he was old enough."

A puzzled look formed on Esme's face. "Old enough for what?"

"One of the first things Proctor did was vaccinate everyone in Utopia against the virus."

"Your people found a cure?"

"Not a cure but a vaccine made from antibodies of those that had been infected. Dr. Carstairs devised it. She was a top doctor before the plague and that's why Proctor treats her with more respect than he shows most women. But there was no way to test it. The vaccine worked but it was flawed. It made the men unable to father children. But

Proctor dreamed of a son: an heir to the empire he was building. He thought he could turn my baby brother into a surrogate son and potential heir. But he couldn't be bothered caring for a little boy. That duty fell to me, along with my other household duties. I had to look after Donjay until he was old enough for Proctor to take him under his wing and groom him to become his heir."

"But this Proctor guy doesn't treat you like his daughter?"

Maga laughed. "Like I said, he doesn't value women. He's never shown any interest or emotion toward me."

"Where's your brother now?"

"Donjay? Probably with Proctor, trying to impress him and earn his praise." Maga sighed.

Proctor looked up at the knock on his door. "Come in." Donjay entered, holding a clipboard. "I'm sorry I barked at you earlier, my boy. I was having a rather frustrating morning but your news has brightened my day. What can I do for you?"

"It's the Humvee, sir. It's on the move." He offered Proctor the latest coordinates.

"Hmm. Perhaps they did manage to find a generator and we haven't located their bunker. We need to be certain. Take a squad of five men to the initial coordinates and investigate. If it's not their bunker, then bring back the generator if you can."

"And if it is the bunker?"

"Report back to me. If there are dozens of teenagers then you'll be outnumbered. We also don't know what their defenses are; if you can determine that it would be useful information."

"Yes sir. Shall I take three Humvees?"

"You'll have to leave them at the perimeter and walk from there. The batteries won't get you that far and back and we can't leave the dome unpatrolled. I want you to send two patrols to converge on the stolen Humvee. It looks like it's heading in our direction. If the stolen Humvee doesn't cross the perimeter then they'll also have to disembark and pursue it by foot once they have a stationary read on it."

"Yes sir. When do you want me to leave?"

"Why, immediately of course, after you've made those arrangements."

"I was hoping I might have time to say goodbye to my sister. Between her schedule and mine, I haven't seen Maga all week."

Proctor gaped. "Oh, yes. Maga. Why don't you wait until you return. If it does turn out to be the bunker then you'll have exciting news to share with her."

Donjay smiled. "Great idea, sir."

"And be careful out there, son." Proctor watched him leave. He stepped down the hall and walked into a laboratory. "Dr. Carstairs."

"Proctor. Did you change your mind about the anxiety pills?"

"No, at least not for me. I may need you to provide some antidepressants to Donjay, however. We've neglected to break the news to him about his sister. I've sent him on a mission; when he returns, I plan to tell him Maga went outside the dome on an errand while he was away and was attacked by wolves. I anticipate that news may cause him some depression for several days. I trust you can devise the proper chemical cocktail to lift his spirits."

"I'm sure I can come up with something."

Chapter Nineteen

"Thank you, Doctor. Get plenty of rest; I think you may soon have a laboratory full of specimens."

Kai sped toward the store, thoroughly enjoying the ride in his not-a-sports-car. He had figured out alternating the amount of pressure on the gas pedal would control the speed of the vehicle and he was now testing how well it could cover different types of terrain. He was disappointed when the small town came into view. He slowed the Humvee to a crawl as he searched for the pane glass window of the store Covid had described. When he sighted it, Kai reluctantly switched off the engine and hopped out of the Humvee. He pulled out several large empty sacks and carried them inside the store.

Kai was overwhelmed by the selection that awaited him. The abandoned store was a virtual treasure trove. Even more intriguing, all of the boxes and tins had colorful pictures on them, unlike the government-manufactured prepackaged foodstuffs with which the bunker had been stocked. He held up some of the cereal boxes and laughed at the imagery on them. He walked from aisle to aisle filling a half-dozen of the large empty sacks, which he then lugged into the Humvee. His shopping trip had taken more than two hours but, to be fair, Kai had to examine each item carefully before placing it into a sack, as he was unfamiliar with all of them. When the last sack had been hefted into the Humvee, he took a final look at the amazing abandoned store and prepared to climb into the vehicle himself. A voice boomed out, "Step away from the Humvee and place your hands in the air."

Startled, Kai looked around to see where the voice had come from. He saw two men with rifles aimed at him standing across the street. He turned to his left and saw two more pointing their guns at him. He glanced to his right and saw another pair of armed men down the road targeting him. Kai didn't know precisely what the rifles were capable of but he remembered being warned by Archer and Robin they shot projectiles. What he didn't know was Proctor had ordered his men to capture anyone in the Humvee unharmed. Kai's eyes darted back and forth as he tried to formulate a plan.

"Put your hands up and surrender." One of the riflemen fired in Kai's direction, striking and shattering the store's plate glass window.

Startled by the flying shards of glass surrounding him, Kai dove beneath the Humvee and climbed into it. The men opened fire on the Humvee, taking care not to aim directly at Kai. "Hey! Quit shooting at my not-a-sports-car!" He scrambled up to the gun turret and grabbed the rifle. "How hard can this be? Just aim it like a bow and arrow and pull the trigger as if releasing an arrow." Kai aimed at the two riflemen across the street and fired. He missed them, understandably as it was his first time firing a rifle. Yet the riflemen didn't know that so they ducked for cover. Kai pivoted, shooting down both sides of the street causing his attackers to scramble. He swiveled the gun against the edge of the turret, firing wildly with a wide grin on his face.

"Not so arrogant now, are you?" Kai called out in-between bursts of gunfire. Then he heard the loud crack of gunshots replaced by a soft clicking sound. "What's wrong with this thing? It's stopped shooting."

All six Utopian riflemen, realizing Kai was out of ammunition, converged on the Humvee.

Chapter Twenty

KAI SCRAMBLED TO CLAMBER INTO the driver's seat. He was about to switch on the engine when he looked up and saw two riflemen standing in front of the Humvee aiming their weapons at him. He glanced in the rearview mirror and saw two more approaching, and the final two targeting him from across the street directly opposite the driver's side of his vehicle.

"This is your last warning. Step out with your hands raised."

Kai knew they could fire before he could start the engine and place the Humvee in Drive. He opened the door and stepped out, holding up his hands. The two riflemen in front of the Humvee took a step toward him. Kai heard a whoosh, as an arrow shot by him and impaled one of them. A split-second later, a second arrow whooshed by, striking the other rifleman in the chest. The pair positioned behind the Humvee pivoted, nervously scanning their surroundings while their trigger fingers tensed. Two more arrows sliced through the air cutting them down. The two gunmen across the street crouched back to back, each firing blindly in the directions the pairs of arrows had come from.

Kai leaped back into the Humvee and started the engine. He swerved left and drove across the road plunging the Humvee directly into them. He backed up the vehicle and placed it in Park, waiting for some sign of his mysterious rescuers.

Archer stepped out several yards in front of the Humvee lowering his bow, while several yards in the opposite direction behind the vehicle Robin appeared, strapping her bow over her shoulder. "Corona was worried about you," Robin said. "Looks like she was right."

"There was no reason for her to be worried. I had the situation completely under control."

Archer slapped him on the back. "Don't worry; we'll be sure to tell her that."

"Do you need a ride back to the bunker?" Kai asked, pondering how he would rearrange the bags of supplies in the Humvee.

"No thanks," Robin said. "We tied our horses about five hundred yards away so we could sneak up on them."

"They look like Utopians," Kai said. "But what were they doing here? We're not near Utopia."

"I don't know but leastways they ain't gonna tell no one about our store now," Robin said.

"We'll have to make more trips to empty the store in case the other Utopians know about it," Archer said.

"I'll fetch our horses," Robin said, returning a few moments later with two horses.

"Thanks for the assist," Kai said, as Archer and Robin mounted them. "Let's head back to the bunker. I'll drive slowly so you can keep up." Kai executed a three-point turn and headed in the direction of the bunker.

Archer turned to Robin and laughed. "Guess he ain't never seen a horse at full gallop before." He smacked his horse's rear and the pair of horses shot off.

Varian stepped into the social area. Although there were few people there — most of the teenagers were outside helping build several structures — Varian pretended not to notice the room emptying as he entered. Fiona had told him it would take time for him to be accepted again but he hadn't realized the degree of antipathy his actions had engendered among his peers. He wondered if there was no one other than Fiona willing to give him a second chance.

"Varian. Just the person I wanted to see."

Varian looked up hopefully. Then, he sighed, his hopefulness dissipating. "Corbin. I should have guessed only you'd speak to me."

"Why, of course I'd speak to you; we have business to conclude. You may recall there's a slight matter of six thousand credits you owe me. I realize you've had an extremely stressful week so I'll waive the interest and late fees."

Varian rolled his eyes. "Look, Corbin, I know I promised you six thousand credits but you may have noticed I'm no longer the bunker's leader and I no longer have access to the cache of casino chips."

"How the mighty have fallen. A short time ago you were our supreme leader, someone to be admired and praised for his principles and integrity. And now, you're lower than a worm, trying to welch on your obligations. Or do you deny your indebtedness to me?"

"I've already admitted I owe you the credits; I simply have no way to pay you."

Corbin shrugged. "That's easily arranged. You can provide a service to me and I'll consider your debt paid in full."

"What sort of service?"

Corbin grinned. "Does it matter? Would you really prefer the alternative: being indebted to me for the rest of your life?"

Varian grimaced. "I won't hurt anyone."

"I wouldn't ask you to."

"All right. What do you want me to do?"

"You once bragged about your ability to pick locks. There's one I want picked. A few minutes of your efforts and you can wipe out a rather large debt."

Varian frowned. "I'm not going to help you steal from anyone."

"I've no intention of stealing from a single living soul. Now come with me and let's get this over with while nearly everyone is still outside the bunker."

Varian sighed. He followed Corbin out of the social area. "Where are we going?"

"You'll see." Corbin led Varian past the sleeping quarters to a seldom-visited section of the bunker.

"What are we doing here? This section's off-limits."

"This section was off-limits." Corbin grinned. "This is the designated living quarters for the grown-ups that were supposed to raise us and care for us. Of course, all but one died in the first few months so only one person has ever lived here for any length of time, and now he's dead too. So technically, we're not trespassing or invading anyone's privacy and there's no one to steal from… No one living, that is. In fact, there's not much here to steal; I know, I've looked."

Chapter Twenty

"So why are we here, Corbin?"

Corbin pointed to the wall. "If someone went to the trouble of installing a wall safe in an underground bunker despite anticipating what might be the end of the world, then I suspect whatever's inside must be of great value. Imagine how frustrated I was when I found I was unable to open the combination lock. And then I thought of you and your self-proclaimed skill at opening locks."

"So what if you find gold or jewels or any stuff people valued before the plague? What good is any of that now? A can of beans would be more valuable."

"Then, at least satisfy my curiosity. It's the mystery that piques my curiosity. Can you open it?"

Varian studied the safe. "Simple tumbler lock. Shouldn't be difficult." He closed his eyes and let his fingers glide across the dial. He stopped when he met resistance and turned the dial in the opposite direction, stopped at the next level of resistance, and dialed it back until he reached the final resistance level. They heard a click and he pulled the door open.

Corbin and Varian peered inside the safe. Varian pulled out what appeared to be a diary. "Looks like this is all there is."

Corbin frowned. "A diary? You can keep it. I've no interest in someone else's memoirs."

"Sorry you didn't find a hidden treasure trove but I did as you requested."

"Yes, yes," he replied annoyedly. "Consider your debt paid in full." Corbin sighed. "It was worth a try."

Varian flipped through the diary. A wide grin filled his face. "Corbin, I take back every miserable thing I've ever thought about you."

Corbin gave him a puzzled look. "I had no idea you'd get so excited over a salacious memoir."

"It's not that kind of diary. It was written by one of the scientists and talks about the bunker. There's a hidden room they didn't want the children to know about that contains a weapons cache. And the bunker itself has an emergency lockdown mechanism and defense grid that can be engaged or disengaged using the coded instructions in this book. I've got to show this to Keiana right away." Varian dashed out of the room leaving a perplexed Corbin behind.

Donjay paused to massage his aching calves. It had been a long walk for quite some miles but he and his five men had reached the outskirts of the encampment being built around the bunker. He motioned for his men to crouch down behind the bushes. "It's a base of some kind," Donjay said. "Hand me your binoculars." He peered through them. "It looks as though they're building the base. They don't appear to be Raiders. They're the age range Proctor said the bunker kids would be. There are too many for us to capture. We need to report back to Proctor and…" Donjay refocused his binoculars. The image came into crystal clarity. There could be no mistake: It was Maga! The bunker kids were holding his sister prisoner.

He had no idea how she might have been captured or when, but Donjay recalled he hadn't seen his sister in about two weeks. He watched as one of teenaged girls grabbed Maga's hand and led her into the bunker. Donjay realized it would be impossible for his small squad to infiltrate the bunker and escape with Maga. He would have to tell Proctor and hope he would launch a rescue mission. Unless they could barter for Maga's freedom. But what would the bunker kids want in exchange for his sister, Donjay wondered. He glanced out and saw two boys approaching and the epiphany struck him.

Maga sat on a boulder watching the others building the base camp atop the bunker. Corona joined her. "How are you settling in?"

Maga shook her head. "I'm not. I have nothing in common with your people. Your lifestyle is so different. In Utopia, I was nowhere near the eldest. I served a function. Here, you've all shared the identical experiences and live by the same code. I feel like an outcast."

"I'm sorry. I guess we take it for granted. But Archer and Robin are also strangers and they've found their function. They've shown us how to shoot arrows, grow crops, ride horses, and build things."

Maga looked around. "I don't see them. Are they down below?"

Corona looked chagrined. "I asked them to do me a favor. I was worried about Kai going to their store alone so I asked Robin and Archer to follow him in case he ran into any trouble."

"The Raiders did that for you?"

"You shouldn't think of them as Raiders. Archer and Robin are just kids like the rest of us."

Maga lowered her head. "Not quite. They're in pain. They've suffered a great loss. I can see that when I observe them. It conflicts with everything I know... everything I've been told about Raiders. They're not the callous, brutal savages we were led to believe. As you say, they're merely children."

"They're also angry. They want vengeance for the deaths of their grandmother and friends. I feel sorry for them. They'll always wonder who killed their grandmother and why. It's a mystery that will haunt them forever."

Maga looked up. "I know who it was."

"How could you possibly? You were with us when it happened."

Maga reached into her pocket and took out the St. Sebastian medal. "I found this on the ground beside the old woman. I know who it belongs to. I've seen it around his neck every day since I first arrived in Utopia."

Corona perused the medal. "It looks familiar. I've seen it before."

"It belongs to Proctor."

"Yes, now I recognize it. But that means... Proctor was at the Outpost!"

"They must have fought. He must not have realized he lost it. Perhaps she ripped it off his neck during a struggle."

"I don't understand," Corona said. "Your people and the Raiders have been enemies for a long time. Why would Proctor attack them now? Archer and Robin said nothing was taken, and of all the Raider outposts one composed of mostly ancient people could hardly be a threat to them."

"I don't know but Proctor never does anything without a reason. He also seldom leads an attack. He usually sends Donjay; he's too cowardly to risk his own life."

"Donjay?"

"My little brother. Proctor treats him like a son."

"We have to show this medal to Archer and Robin when they return."

"They'll hate me even more when they learn it was the Utopians who slaughtered their outpost."

Corona shook her head. "No, they'll thank you for giving them closure. In the meantime, we should show this to Covid." She called out, "Covid! Has anyone seen Covid?"

"He said he was going to speak to Keiana when I saw earlier inside the bunker," Corbin said.

"Thanks, Corbin." Corona grabbed Maga's hand and led her into the bunker. "Come on, let's find him."

"Hey, Corbin!" Tristan shouted. "Give me a hand with this irrigation piping."

Corbin walked several yards away from the base camp to join Tristan. "What are you doing?"

"Setting up irrigation for the garden. We can't rely on rain for the crops. Grab one of these pipes we made and follow me."

Corbin reluctantly lifted the pipe. "How far are we going?"

"About a quarter mile to the lake we discovered. We're going to lay out these pipes and connect them from the lake to the garden. Archer has a pump back at the Outpost he's going to retrieve later. In a few months we'll have grown more food than you can imagine."

"Do you know how long it'll take to carry enough pipes one at a time?" Corbin asked, hefting the pipe along the path.

"That's why we're taking them to the lake: the more we bring there, the shorter the return trips with each succeeding pipe."

Corbin spotted the lake ahead. "Still, there must be an easier way. Can't these things be loaded into Kai's not-a-sports-car?"

"Kai's using it to make runs back and forth to the store. Besides, what else were you planning to do? It's a beautiful day outside. The weather's perfect and it beats another day inside the bunk—" Tristan had the breath knocked out of him as two Utopian men tackled him and cuffed his hands behind his back. Three other Utopians pounced on Corbin and did the same to him, gagging both boys. The men dragged them to their feet.

Donjay unholstered his pistol and aimed it at Corbin's temple. "Proctor wants all of you alive but I only need one of you. I'll shoot the first one who tries to escape. Understand?"

Corbin nodded vigorously; Tristan nodded as well.

"Good," Donjay said. "We have a long walk back to our Humvees." He smiled. *Proctor will be pleased to have a replacement for the boy who escaped*, he thought. *And we'll have one boy left to barter for Maga's release.*

Chapter Twenty-One

W ITH MOST OF THE TEENAGERS setting up the base camp outside on the surface, Varian hardly needed to close the library door to ensure privacy, yet he had anyway. Destine and Keiana's eyes widened as they perused the diary Varian had shown them. "You're the two smartest people in the bunker," he said. "What do you make of it?"

"It's incredible!" Keiana said.

"Not really," Destine said. "It makes sense the military would include a cache of weapons when they designed it so the bunker wouldn't be defenseless against any hostile survivors. It also makes sense the adults never told us about it while we were growing up because there was no reason to expose children in a presumably safe environment to dangerous weapons."

"I was referring to the defense grid and the automatic lockdown mechanism," Keiana said. "It must be controlled by a computer somehow tied in to the generators. Since we've never seen any computers anywhere in the bunker outside of references in books in the library, I had always assumed there were no functioning computers left."

"Can you two read up on computers so you can figure out how to operate the lockdown mechanism and the defense grid, assuming we can locate this computer?" Varian asked.

"Of course," Keiana said.

"Meanwhile, I'll search for the computer," Varian said.

"You can't search the entire bunker by yourself," Destine said. "Get Dax and Ian to help you. I'll talk to Covid. He and Corona can look for the weapons cache. Kai can help when he returns."

"Don't tell anyone other than those six," Keiana said. "They're the most responsible individuals. The last thing we want is some immature kid stumbling onto them and tampering with the computer or the weapons as if they were toys."

"All right, you two hit the computer books," Varian said. "I'll find Covid and send him here, and then recruit Dax and Ian." Varian left the library, as Keiana and Destine scanned the shelves for computer how-to books.

Proctor looked up as Dr. Carstairs entered his office. "How are the preparations coming?"

"If you're seriously anticipating more than a dozen teenagers arriving from the hidden bunker then I suggest you increase the guards and keep any new arrivals chained so they don't escape the way Kai and Corona did."

Proctor nodded. "There's no longer any advantage to subtlety. Kai and Corona have undoubtedly shared their experiences in Utopia with their companions. Any that we capture will seek to escape immediately. We may even retrieve Kai and Corona if they're the ones in the stolen

Humvee we're tracking. Our men should have intercepted them by now."

Dr. Carstairs grimaced, raising her hand to her throat. "If so, I'll personally deal with the girl and make her suffer for what she did to me."

Donjay stepped through the door. "Excuse me, Proctor."

"Ah, Donjay. You're back. What news do you bring from your surveillance excursion? Was it the bunker or merely a stray generator?"

Donjay smiled. "We found the hidden bunker and the kids are still there. They're even building some structures on the ground above the bunker. Other than a watchtower, I saw no visible defenses."

"Excellent news. How many inhabitants are there?"

"Hard to say. About three dozen outside, maybe more inside the bunker. They didn't see us but I was able to capture two males that strayed from their camp."

Proctor was ecstatic. He threw his arms around Donjay. "My boy, I could not be prouder of you if you were my own flesh and blood. You see, Dr. Carstairs? This is the future of Utopia."

"Proctor, there's something else," Donjay began. "Maga—"

"Ah, yes," Proctor cut him off. "About Maga. I'm afraid I have some bad news for you. While you were away, Maga left the dome on an errand for Dr. Carstairs. She was hardly a few yards from the dome when she was set upon by a stray pack of ferocious wolves. It happened so fast there was nothing anyone could do."

"Wolves?" Donjay said. "It must have been someone else; it can't have been Maga."

Proctor placed his hand on Donjay's shoulder. "I know how difficult it must be to hear this and accept your sister's death, but there's no question of her demise. Dr. Carstairs observed the whole tragedy and I positively identified the remains beyond any doubt. I won't describe the gruesome details but I assure you it was Maga."

He's lying, Donjay thought. *I just left Maga at the bunker. But why does he want me to believe Maga's dead?* "That's... shocking to hear."

"I must say, you're taking this better than I had expected. I'm enormously proud of you today, son. Send in your prisoners and then return to your duties. See Dr. Carstairs if you feel the need for any antidepressants to help cope with this unpleasant news."

"That won't be necessary." Donjay left the room, gesturing for his men waiting in the hall to escort Tristan and Corbin into Proctor's office.

"You see, Dr. Carstairs? I've raised a fine specimen of Utopian manhood."

Dr. Carstairs frowned. "Perhaps, although I would have expected a more emotional reaction." She shrugged. "The boy may still be in shock."

"Go prepare your laboratory, Doctor. Thanks to Donjay, you'll have new subjects sooner than anticipated." Dr. Carstairs nodded and left. Corbin and Tristan were ushered into Proctor's office. The guards stepped back, leaving the two bound boys standing side by side as Proctor circled them, perusing them from head to toe. "You're younger than Kai. How old are you?"

"Fourteen," Tristan said. "You'd better let us go or our friends will come looking for us."

"Really?" Proctor chuckled. "That would be most convenient. It would save me the trouble of having to collect them. But either way, they'll all soon be joining you.

Fourteen, you say? Not yet at your prime but that means you'll be consistent producers for years to come." He turned to one of the guards. "Take them to the laboratory. Tell Dr. Carstairs I want a full medical report on each of them before we begin the extraction process." The guards approached the boys.

"Wait!" Corbin exclaimed. "I have something you want."

Proctor took a step closer to Corbin. "And what might that be?"

Corbin glanced at the guards before returning his gaze to Proctor. "Do you really want your gossiping men overhearing your private conversations?"

Proctor grinned. "Is this a plan to be alone with me so you can overpower me and escape?"

Corbin smirked. "I thought you were more intelligent than that."

Proctor slapped his face, sending Corbin hurtling to the floor.

"Are you afraid to be alone with a fifteen-year-old boy? Do you think I can overpower you with my wrists handcuffed behind my back? I can't even open a door, let alone get past the guards, escape a domed city, or return home on foot."

Proctor watched the boy struggle to his feet. "You intrigue me." He turned to the guards. "Leave us. Take the other one to the laboratory. And close the door behind you." Proctor waited until the door was shut. "You've piqued my curiosity. But I warn you: choose your next words carefully. Waste my time and I shall introduce you to tortures even your nightmares have yet to conceive of."

"Your bootlicker said you want all of us captured unharmed. We must be quite valuable to you — but only if

211

you can capture everyone in the bunker alive. I know them: they'll defend it with their lives. If you attack, not only will some of your men be lost but at least half of those in the bunker will be killed."

Proctor rubbed his chin. "Regrettable, but I'll still capture a dozen or two. Not ideal, but acceptable."

"How would you like all forty-eight, unharmed, with no losses on your side?"

"You continue to intrigue me, boy. Go on."

"I want to cut a deal."

"For your freedom and that of your friend, I assume?"

Corbin shrugged. "I doubt he would agree to the terms, just as I doubt you'd release both your prisoners. You hold him to make sure I keep my end of the bargain."

"Which is?"

"The bunker was built by the military. It's a massive underground structure with a six-inch titanium hatch. The military didn't plan to leave fifty kids defenseless: there's an automatic lockdown mechanism and a defense grid."

Proctor arched his eyebrows. "A defense grid? Tell me about it."

"There's a book containing the notes and documentation. I only flipped through it — something to do with satellites and targeting. Too complex for a fifteen-year-old like me to grasp."

"I'm beginning to think you're a fifteen-year-old whom it would be a mistake to underestimate."

"The book contains the codes to engage and disengage the system. With those codes, you could shut down their defenses, walk right in and capture them all."

"Does the book also contain the passwords to enable us to hack into the bunker's computer?"

"Since it's the only record of the bunker's defense system, I'd assume it contains everything you would need to know. Of course, the only way to find out is to read the book. Would you like me to get it for you?"

Proctor grinned. "An interesting proposition, And what do you get out of the deal?"

"One of your vehicles, fully charged and packed with supplies and weapons. If I have to flee my home, then I want everything I'll need to survive on my own."

"You'd sacrifice your companions so cavalierly?"

"I'm keeping half of them from being slaughtered in a battle with your forces that they can't win. I'm doing them a favor, although I doubt they'd see it that way."

"You needn't flee and wander the earth like a Nomad. I like your style. You may reside in Utopia with all the privileges of citizenship."

"That would be a honor, coming as it does from a man with whom I feel I share similar traits... Which is why I can't accept your considerate offer. We're too much alike: I don't trust you. I'll settle for the vehicle and supplies."

Proctor laughed. "By that reasoning, I shouldn't trust you, either."

"Except you have nothing to lose. You'll still have one boy and a chance to capture everyone. If I betray you and remain at the bunker, you'll attack and I'll either be killed or recaptured. I have no incentive not to carry out my end of the deal, while you have everything to gain and nothing to lose. Which will it be?"

"Very well." Proctor summoned Donjay, who entered momentarily. "Donjay will equip you with a stocked Humvee and drive you to the perimeter. From there, return to the bunker and acquire the codebook. Rejoin Donjay at the perimeter and you may exchange the book for the vehicle. Donjay will have to walk back to Utopia until one of our patrols spots him and picks him up."

Corbin smiled. "Then, we have a deal?"

Proctor nodded and directed Donjay to unlock Corbin's handcuffs. Corbin rubbed his sore wrists. He hesitated, then asked, "What will happen to Tristan?"

"Tristan?"

"The other boy."

"Oh." Proctor said. "Does it matter?"

Corbin looked down. He raised his head, staring directly into Proctor's eyes. "No. Not really."

Donjay parked the Humvee. "This is as far as we go. I'll wait here at the perimeter."

"Undoubtedly a good idea," Corbin said. "Any farther and they might spot your vehicle from the watchtower." He opened the passenger door.

Donjay placed his hand on Corbin's shoulder. "Wait."

Corbin's pulse quickened. He wondered if Donjay might be a variable he hadn't accounted for in his scheming. "What?"

"Your people are holding one of ours prisoner."

Corbin cocked his head. "What?"

"A girl. Her name's Maga."

"Ah, Maga. I've seen her around the bunker. But no one's holding her prisoner. She's free to leave whenever she wishes."

Now it was Donjay's turn to look surprised. "If she's not being held against her will, then why...?"

"You'd have to ask her."

Donjay grimaced. "I will. Send her to me."

Corbin sighed. "I suppose I could give her your message and describe where to find you. I can't force her to come, though."

"Tell her Donjay wants to see her."

Corbin shrugged. "I could do that. But what's in it for me?"

"What do you want?"

Corbin perused Donjay. "Your pistol."

Donjay frowned and pointed to the back seat. "You'll be getting a satchel full of weapons when you return."

"Yes, but I never do a deal without taking something of value; and you have nothing to offer other than your clothes and your sidearm. I can see how highly you value your gun... although it might be amusing to add your clothes to the deal."

Frustrated, Donjay handed him the gun. "Here. I still have the other weapons in the satchel. Now send Maga to me."

Corbin accepted the gun, examining it closely. "So all I do is point and squeeze this?" He wrapped his finger around the trigger and aimed the gun at Donjay's head. He saw the fear in Donjay's eyes. "Not very smart, are you?" Corbin lowered the gun. "Fortunately for you, I never welch on a deal. I'll tell Maga you're waiting here." He stepped out of the Humvee. He glanced down at the wet spot that had formed on Donjay's pants. "If you wait in the sun, that may dry quicker." Corbin chuckled and headed back to the bunker.

Chapter Twenty-Two

THE NOT-A-SPORTS-CAR ROARED INTO VIEW of the base camp, followed by a pair of horseback riders. "Hail the conquering heroes!" Kai called out. Several teens surrounded the Humvee, unloading the supplies. Covid and Corona raced up to them.

"You'll have to postpone your next shopping trip," Covid said. "Something's come up."

Kai cocked his head. "What is it?"

"We need you to help us look for a secret computer terminal. But first, Corona and I need to talk to Archer and Robin." The siblings glanced at each other and dismounted.

"Ain't got tired of having us 'round already, has you?" Archer asked.

"Of course not," Corona said. She pulled out Proctor's St. Sebastian medal and showed it to them. "Maga found this at the Outpost near Granny's body."

Robin studied it. "Ain't never seen her wear that before."

"It's not Granny's," Covid said. "It belongs to Proctor, the leader of the Utopians."

"What would Granny be doing with a Utopian's medal?" Archer asked.

Robin's face contorted in a paroxysm of rage. "Ain't no reason 'less'en it fell off the man that killed her."

Archer frowned. "We're gonna need some fresh horses."

Robin checked her quiver. "And some more arrows."

"Wait!" Kai exclaimed. "You two aren't thinking of going to Utopia by yourselves, are you?"

"We ain't looking fer a fight with the Utopians," Archer said. "Just this fella named Proctor. Long as none of 'em try to stop us from killing Proctor, we'll leave 'em like we found 'em."

"Have you ever been to Utopia?" Kai asked. "I have. They have patrols circling the dome in vehicles like my not-a-sports-car."

"Granny done taught us how to hunt in stealth," Robin said. "They won't see us coming."

"They've got rifles," Kai said.

"So did the ones we just killed," Archer said.

"The city's covered with a freaking dome!" Kai said.

"Gotta be a way in and out," Archer said. "We'll find it."

"I met Proctor. He's merciless."

"That's good, 'cause we won't be showing him none," Robin said.

"The not-a-sports-car needs to recharge. I can have it ready to go in the morning."

"Kai," Covid said. "We need you here. We must find—"

"Archer and Robin saved my skin at the store today. I'm going with them to Utopia."

Archer placed his hand on Kai's shoulder. "Robin and I really appreciate that, Kai. But this here's something we got to do ourselves. Fer Granny."

Kai gaped. "But you'll probably get killed."

"Could be," Robin said. "But like my brother said, this is family business we got to settle."

Corona sighed. "If you need any of our supplies…"

"All we're gonna need's some fresh horses and a lot more arrows," Robin said. "But thanks, anyway. We'll be back soon." She turned to Covid. "'Course, if'n we don't make it back, there's something I been meaning to tell you." She leaned in as if to whisper in his ear and instead kissed him on the lips. "Couldn't find the words so that'll have to do."

Archer shook his head. "You tryin' to give our friends the plague?"

"I ain't infected and there ain't no plague no more anyway. You collect the horses while I get us a few quivers."

Covid stood speechless as they walked away. Corona smiled at him. "Looks like you're going to have to continue that conversation when they return."

Kai frowned. "If they come back."

Corbin tucked the handgun into his waistband and covered it with his shirt. He wasn't sure if he might need to use it one day or if it might prove valuable barter in some future transaction. He looked around the camp for Maga and not seeing her he descended into the bunker. Corbin found her cleaning the social area. "I didn't realize they had assigned you to the chores rotation yet."

Maga looked up sheepishly. "I hope I'm not displacing someone. Old habits die hard, I guess. I feel more relaxed doing what I used to do in Utopia."

"That's sort of what I wanted to talk to you about. I'm Corbin. We met briefly last week."

"I remember. You asked if there was anything you could do for me and added your rates were very reasonable."

"And that's why I'm here. I have a message for you. A friend of yours wants you to meet him."

Magda looked puzzled. "I don't have any friends in the bunker."

Corbin shook his head. "One of your pals from Utopia."

Maga turned ashen. "They've found me!"

"Not '*they*'; it's one boy. He said to tell you Donjay wants to see you."

"Donjay!" Maga sighed in relief. "He came alone? Are you certain?"

"Absolutely. He's waiting for you a few miles away in a vehicle like Kai's not-a-sports-car. I can point out the path for you."

"Oh, yes, please!"

They stepped outside and Kai led her to the path. "This will lead straight to him." He paused. "You sure you want to go?"

Maga nodded. "I trust Donjay. He's the only one I do trust. Thank you, Corbin."

Corbin watched her head along the path, wondering if he had done the right thing. Then, he returned to the bunker to search for the codebook.

Donjay leaped out of the Humvee when he saw Maga approach. "Maga!"

"Donjay!" She rushed to him. "What are you doing out here?"

"I should be asking you that. Proctor told me you had been eaten by wolves. What's going on, Maga?"

Chapter Twenty-Two

"I ran away from Utopia. Dr. Carstairs threatened to send me to the farm."

"She must have been joking."

"She was deadly serious. She blamed me for allowing her prisoner to escape. If I go back, she'll have me killed."

"Proctor won't allow—"

"Proctor doesn't care about me, Donjay. He was willing to let Dr. Carstairs send me to the farm."

Donjay shook his head. "No, he wouldn't..."

"He told you I was eaten by wolves? If I had stayed, I'd have been eaten by Dr. Carstairs!"

"Why would he lie to me?"

"Proctor has lied about everything. The bunker kids gave me shelter. Even the Raiders helped me, before Proctor slaughtered them. None of them need to be our enemies; Proctor made them that."

"But... he's grooming me to take his place."

"Do you honestly think that will ever happen? Proctor will never cede power and it'll be a long time before he dies of old age. If you fall out of favor between now and then, he'll send you to the farm."

"I'm confused."

"Come back with me. The bunker kids will welcome you."

Donjay thought of Corbin... and of Tristan. "No, they won't. Besides, I need to confront Proctor." He pointed to a tree. "Tell Corbin to leave the book at the base of the tree. I'll come back for it."

"What book?"

"He'll know. Tell him to forget about the Humvee: the battery charge will die when it crosses the perimeter. Proctor lied to him, too. He never intended for Corbin to get away."

He placed his hands on her shoulders. "I'll send for you when it's safe for you to return to Utopia."

"Be careful, Donjay. Proctor's more dangerous than you believe him to be."

He kissed her forehead. "I love you, big sister."

"I love you, too." Maga watched Donjay walk back toward Utopia until her brother became a speck on the horizon. Then, she returned to the bunker.

Corona and Covid entered the library excitedly. "We found the weapons cache," Corona told Destine and Keiana. "There's a hidden panel in one of the storerooms."

"Rifles, grenades, and other stuff I didn't recognize," Covid said. "I think some of it might be explosives. The rest I can't even guess at."

"We'll take a look and try to match it with photos in the military books," Destine said. "The most important task now is locating the computer terminal that controls the defense grid."

"Any word from Dax, Ian, or Varian?" Covid asked.

Keiana shook her head. "I assume they're still looking."

"How's the research coming?" Corona asked.

"If the computer terminal has a user-friendly interface, then we should be able to enter the codes and access the defense grid," Keiana said.

"And if not?" Covid asked.

"If not," Destine said, "we'll have to determine what computer language was used to create the program and then become proficient in that language — assuming the library contains a book on the particular language they used."

"And assuming we can learn enough of it from a book, if such a book exists," Keiana said. "Otherwise, when we find the terminal we could simply experiment."

"Trial and error with a defense grid?" Covid asked. "You might blow us up."

"I suggested that possibility," Destine said, "But, as is her typical fashion, in her legendary hubris Keiana has assured me that won't happen."

Covid sighed. "Keep up the good work. Keiana, no trial and error without Destine's agreement, all right?"

"Fine," Keiana said reluctantly. "Just find that terminal."

Varian stood in what they had long ago referred to as "the grownup quarters." *It has to be here,* he thought. *We've searched everywhere else. It makes sense they would keep a computer terminal where only the adults could access it: so where is it?* He grew frustrated and kicked the floor rug. Then, he silently cursed himself for losing his temper and dropped to his knees to straighten the throw rug. Varian felt something beneath the rug. He whipped it away. "A trapdoor!" He pulled on the panel until it opened, revealing a staircase. "Who would think to look for a hidden subterranean room beneath an underground bunker?" Varian descended the staircase.

Varian stepped into the secret room and gasped. The lights, apparently connected to sensors and powered by the generators, came on automatically when he entered the room. He saw multiple computer terminals lined up in a row. "I've got to get Destine and Keiana in here to see this. Hopefully they'll know how to work this stuff."

He climbed back up and replaced the trapdoor and throw rug. Varian heard footsteps and hid behind the door. *No one's allowed in this area: do the footsteps belong to one of those searching for the computer or someone else trespassing?* Varian wondered.

The door gradually, surreptitiously, opened and a figure stepped inside. Varian slammed the door shut behind it as the figure stepped into the light. "Corbin!"

"Varian. Just the person I wanted to see."

"What are you doing here? This is a restricted area."

Corbin smiled. "And yet, here you are. It looks as though we're both bad at following rules. Perhaps Kai's been a bad influence on us."

"You haven't answered my question. Why are you here?"

"The codebook I found: I want it back."

"Forget it, Corbin. That diary's the only thing that can save the bunker."

"Nothing can save the bunker. The Utopians are planning to attack us. They have an entire city, military vehicles, trained troops and weapons. We're a bunch of kids sitting in a hole in the ground."

"How do you know the Utopians are planning an attack?"

"Their head guy Proctor told me himself."

Varian's jaw dropped. "You've been to Utopia?"

"Tristan and I were kidnapped. The Utopians are still holding him prisoner. I can use the codebook to barter for his freedom and you can use the time to evacuate the bunker. Flee while you have the chance."

"You expect me to believe you'd risk your life to save Tristan or anyone else? What's your real game, Corbin?"

"I was going to flee myself. I have a Utopian vehicle loaded with supplies and weapons waiting for me. But there was one nagging detail: Tristan was still in the hands of the Utopians. That irked me."

"Will wonders never cease? You have a conscience, after all?"

"Don't be insulting. I have an ego and a talent for deal-making. I believe I can use the codebook to finagle Tristan's release without putting myself in danger. As long as I have something Proctor wants badly, I'm in control of the situation."

"Don't be stupid. No matter how clever you think you are, you're still a kid. Proctor's a grown man, and from what Kai has told me, he can't be trusted."

"Your lack of confidence in my abilities is duly noted. Now give me the diary."

"I don't have it."

"Then, take me to it."

"No."

"We don't have time to argue." Corbin pulled out the gun from his waistband and pointed it at Varian. "This device is called a gun."

"I know what it is."

"Then you know you don't want me to use it. I want the book."

Varian took a step toward him. "You won't shoot me, Corbin."

Corbin cocked his head. "Do you really believe that, Varian?"

"You're a schemer and a petty thief but you're not a killer."

"I'm a survivor… I'll do whatever it takes to survive. And right now, that means using the diary for barter. Don't test me, Varian."

Varian stepped up to Corbin until the gun was level with his chest. Corbin's mouth twitched, the tremors causing his jaw to quiver. He tightened his finger on the trigger as the shaking reached his head. His eyes welled up with tears and he thrust the gun to his side. "Damn you, Varian."

"Congratulations. You passed the test." Varian pointed to the floor. "Now give me a hand moving this rug."

Puzzled and confused, Corbin knelt and pulled the rug away, revealing the trapdoor. "What—?"

"The secret room containing the computer terminals that control the defense grid. Keiana and Destine are studying how to operate computers. When you show them this, they can use the defense grid to protect the bunker and possibly even obliterate Utopia."

Corbin stood open-jawed. "We actually have a chance?"

"More than a chance."

"Wait. You want *me* to be the one to tell them about the room?"

"We can't leave one of us in Utopia, especially if we can use these weapon systems to attack their city. Someone's got to rescue Tristan and you've just proved you're no fighter."

Corbin's eyes widened. "You're going after him? But he hates you."

"He's one of us. I promised to keep everyone safe."

Corbin shook his head. "You're not the leader anymore. You don't have to—"

"I'm not *the* leader anymore. But I was born to be *a* leader."

Corbin thought back to Maga's words earlier. "Old habits die hard." He handed Varian the gun. "You may need this."

"Thanks." Varian slipped the gun into his waistband. "What do I owe you for it?"

Corbin shook his head. "Paid in full."

Varian turned to leave.

"Good luck," Corbin added.

Varian looked back, nodded, and left.

Chapter Twenty-Three

VARIAN RACED THROUGH THE SUBTERRANEAN complex, running into Kai and Corona. "Where are you going in such a hurry?" Corona asked.

"We found the computer terminal," Varian gasped, catching his breath. "There's a trapdoor in the grownups' quarters; Corbin's there now."

"Then, I don't need to keep searching," Kai said. "I can go to Utopia to help Archer and Robin."

"They said they wanted to confront Proctor alone," Corona said.

"I know," Kai said. "But that doesn't mean I'm going to stand by and let them be killed. You know I've never been good at doing what I'm told." He kissed her goodbye.

"I'm going to Utopia, too," Varian said. "The Utopians kidnapped Corbin and Tristan. Corbin escaped to get help for Tristan."

"I'll tell Covid and Ian, and we'll join you," Corona said.

"No," Varian said. "Stay here and help Destine and Keiana get the computer up and running. Proctor knows the bunker's location and an attack is imminent. We'll need all of you here to protect the bunker." He turned to Kai. "Can we use your vehicle?"

"It won't be recharged until morning. We can take a couple of horses from the corral; I'll also bring a bow and quiver."

Varian nodded. "Then, let's go." The two boys headed to the exit hatch.

"Be careful!" Corona called out after them.

Destine and Keiana stared in awe at the computer terminals. "It's amazing!" Destine said. "Like a picture book come to life."

"Can you make it work?" Covid asked.

Keiana glowered at him. "Give us a chance to turn it on first. There must be a switch somewhere."

Destine pressed a button and the row of terminals lit up.

Keiana frowned. "What happened to no trial and error, you'll blow everything up?"

Destine gave her a smug smile. "It worked, didn't it?"

"Now what?" Covid asked.

"We wait for it to come online." Destine held up the codebook. "Hopefully, it'll ask for the password and then for the codes."

"And if it doesn't?"

"Wait, it's coming," Destine said. "Yes! I'm typing in the password… now it wants the codes." The screen flickered on each of the terminals and was replaced by a topographical map.

"I recognize that terrain," Covid said. "That's the bunker… and to the north is Utopia."

Chapter Twenty-Three

"The computer's communicating with a satellite in geosynchronous orbit, 22,236 miles above the Earth," Destine said.

"Multiple satellites, actually," Keiana said. "The defense grid includes surveillance satellites, long-range sensors, and short-range targeting systems."

"What does that mean?" Covid asked.

"It means once we figure out how to activate the grid we'll be able to defend ourselves and employ limited offensive capabilities," Keiana said.

Destine pointed to the map. "There are high-tech landmines dispersed throughout the immediate surface area. We'll be able to detonate them individually or in a random sequence. We'll also be able to fire two dozen pop-up missile launchers."

"Pop-up missile launchers?"

Destine nodded. "Hidden below the ground, they pop up when ready to be fired. Even more pop-up automated rifles that can crisscross the area outside the bunker. Remember, this entire place was built by the military."

"Once we master the controls, the bunker should be as well protected as any military base was before the plague," Keiana said.

"How long will that take you?" Covid asked.

Keiana shrugged. "With luck, a few hours. Otherwise, a few years."

Covid frowned. "Corbin believes Proctor's attack is imminent. Try to get this working but in case you can't, I'm going to have Dax and Ian distribute the weapons cache. If Proctor's men are sighted from the watchtower, we'll have to fight them off." Covid ascended the staircase to the bunker.

Covid, Corona, Dax, and Ian transported the weapons cache to the social area where the remaining teens had gathered. "The attack could come at any time," Covid said. "We'll institute daily training drills, starting today, but our information leads us to believe the Utopians may attack within the next seventy-two hours so you each must be ready to defend yourselves and our home."

Nessa squeezed Fiona's hand. "I don't like the thought of having to harm people," Fiona said.

"It beats them harming you," Dax said, familiarizing herself with the weapon she had been given.

Coralie gazed up at Dax. "Do you think we can beat them?"

Dax nodded. "No doubt in my mind. Especially if we take the fight to them. Between these weapons and the defense grid Covid told us about, we can do more than protect the bunker — we can attack Utopia."

"If we get those missiles working, we can turn Utopia into a pile of rubble," Ian said.

"No!" Maga's heart jumped. She pulled Covid aside. "You can't attack Utopia."

"I hope it doesn't come to that," Covid said. "But they're planning to attack us. They're already holding Tristan prisoner, and Kai and Varian are on their way to rescue him. If we lose three of our people I suspect the others won't rest until Utopia's destroyed."

"My brother's gone back to the city. He could be injured or killed in an attack."

"I'm sorry. As I said, I hope it doesn't come to that. But we're fighting for our lives. It was the Utopians who

230

kidnapped my sister and Kai, and later Tristan and Corbin. And it was the Utopians who killed Archer and Robin's grandmother and friends."

"I have to warn my brother."

"I can't let you reveal our defenses to them."

"You know I don't want to help Proctor. He'd likely have me killed if he saw me. But I want to save my brother just as you would do the same to save your sister. Let me bring Donjay back here to live in the bunker. Please, Covid. I won't betray you. I only want to keep my baby brother alive."

Covid sighed. "Take one of the horses if you think you can ride well enough. You'll both be welcome here."

"Thank you." Maga dashed out of the social area toward the exit hatch.

"That was foolish," Dax said. "You've endangered us all."

"No," Corona said. "I trust Maga. Covid and I understand the attachment between siblings. I also know she'd never help the people trying to kill her. Is it so hard for you to understand wanting to protect someone you love?"

Dax glanced at Coralie and returned her gaze to Corona. "I hope you're right."

Proctor looked up when Donjay entered the room. "Tell me you have the codebook."

"Not yet. Corbin has gone to the bunker to procure it."

"Why aren't you waiting in the Humvee for him to return with it, as we planned?"

"I needed to speak to you. Don't worry; I sent him a message to leave the codebook at a specific location where I can retrieve it."

"A message? How could you send a message to someone in the bunker?"

"I asked my sister to deliver it." Donjay saw the surprise register on Proctor's face. "She's been living at the bunker. Apparently, she wasn't eaten by wolves. And even more apparently, you lied to me."

Proctor grimaced. "She had fled Utopia. I thought it best for you to have closure, rather than wondering if she were dead or alive."

"Maga told me she fled because Dr. Carstairs had planned to send her to the farm… with your approval."

"You're becoming far too emotional over a female. Your sister's only a maid; like nearly all females, she has no significant value to our society."

"Maga's my sister — she has value to me!"

"If you wish to sit in my chair one day and rule Utopia, then you must rid yourself of sentiment and nostalgic childhood attachments. A week ago, I grasped my mother's throat and throttled the life from her weary bones. My mother, your sister — like all females, useful only for breeding or household tasks. I see you still have much to learn. If you've said anything to Maga then the security of our plan has been compromised. That means it's time for Plan B."

"What are you talking about?"

"We proceed without the codebook; for all we know, Corbin may have been lying about it and the so-called defense system anyway. Instead, we'll overrun the bunker and capture them through brute force. I've already ordered half of our Humvees to be equipped with spare batteries from the other half. While it means fifty percent of our Humvees will be idled, the rest will have sufficient power to reach the bunker and return."

"You'd leave Utopia defenseless?"

Chapter Twenty-Three

"Only for a few hours. By nightfall, the bunker shall be ours and the patrols will once again be roaming the perimeter."

"Even though they're children, they'll still resist. We could be facing a siege that lasts for days."

Proctor shook his head. "Once they watch their friends die they'll lose their taste for battle. It's regrettable we'll have to sacrifice some of them, but—"

"Maga's at the bunker. She could be killed in that type of assault."

Proctor shrugged. "If so, she'd merely be collateral damage." He called out for his guards and two entered. "Restrain Donjay." They each grabbed Donjay's arms.

"What are you doing?" Donjay cried.

Dr. Carstairs entered the room.

"Perfect timing, Doctor. I'm afraid Donjay has become agitated and requires a sedative. My men will escort him to your laboratory so you may administer a mild one to him."

The men pulled Donjay away. "Why are you doing this to me?"

"I don't want you mistakenly making a rash emotional decision in your anxious state that might interfere with my plan. Dr. Carstairs will make sure you're too tired and sluggish to be tempted to do anything we might both regret. I'll see you later this evening."

Donjay struggled as the two guards led him out, followed by Dr. Carstairs.

Kai and Varian approached the Utopian perimeter. "Wait until that patrol moves on," Varian said.

Kai squinted. "I can't see what they're doing but it hasn't moved in a while. I'll ride in for a closer look."

"I said to stay put."

"And I flouted your orders back when you were in charge; what makes you think I'd follow them now?" Kai spurred his horse to trot forward.

Reluctantly, Varian did the same.

"There's two of them in the vehicle slumped over," Kai said. They trotted nearer and saw arrows sticking out of the men. "Archer and Robin came this way."

"We need to break Tristan out before they try to kill Proctor and all hell breaks loose."

"I remember where they held me captive the first day. If we don't run into any more patrols, I can lead us there."

Kai and Varian tied their horses to a tree and made their way to the dome entrance. "It's strange," Kai said. "There were a lot more patrols when Corona and I escaped, yet we've only encountered the same one Robin and Archer did."

Varian frowned. "That's not good."

"Of course it is; otherwise we'd have been caught."

"That's not what I meant. If the patrols aren't where they should be, then where are they?" Varian saw the epiphany flicker in Kai's eyes.

"They've begun mounting their attack!" Kai exclaimed.

"As soon as we rescue Tristan, we must warn the others."

"You take Tristan back to the bunker. I'll make sure Archer and Robin come back, too."

"I'm not rescuing Tristan only to lose you. For once in your life, just follow directions."

"Sorry, Tyrant King. I don't even follow directions on a can of soup." He stroked his bow. "Archer taught me how to use this; I plan to show him how well I've learned."

"And all this time I thought Covid was the sanctimonious hero." Varian sighed. "Try not to get yourself killed."

Chapter Twenty-Three

Kai nodded. "The mansion they kept me in is close to the dome entrance. If Tristan's not in Dr. Carstairs lab, then he'll probably be in the same bedroom they put me in, or worse, the Dairy. Follow me." Kai led Varian into the city and to Proctor's mansion. Once inside, they crept furtively down the hallway. Kai pointed to a door. "That's the bedroom they kept me in, and the next one's where they kept Corona."

"We'll check them both," Varian said. "Guard the hall." Kai drew his bow and notched an arrow, placing his back to the door. Varian slowly turned the doorknob, gently inching the door open while hoping the hinges wouldn't creak. He saw the back of a guard's head as he sat facing the bed while reading a book. Tristan lay on the bed, one wrist handcuffed to the bedpost. Varian pulled Corbin's gun from his waistband and pushed the door wide enough to pass through. He slipped behind the guard and placed the gun barrel against the back of his head. "I have a gun pointed at your head. If you move too quickly, it may go off."

The guard froze. Tristan sat up, surprised. Varian noticed the handcuffs.

"Do you have the key?"

"Yes," the guard said, perspiration beading on his forehead.

"If you unlock the handcuffs and trade places with Tristan then I won't have to kill you. Or, I can shoot you and take the key from your dead body. Which way are we doing this?"

"I'll be sent to the farm if I let the prisoner escape."

"You're talking about your future; you won't have one if you don't." He poked the barrel into the guard's head. "This gun's getting heavy. Do I have to decide for you?"

"All right! Don't shoot." He stood and walked toward the bed.

"Slowly, now. I want to see everything you do."

The guard unlocked the cuff around Tristan's wrist. The boy jumped off the bed and ran to Varian.

"Now, place it on your wrist. I didn't hear it click. That's better." Varian replaced the gun in his waistband and turned to Tristan. "Are you all right?"

"Yeah. How did you know—?"

"Corbin. He made it back to the bunker."

Tristan stared at Varian in disbelief. "You risked your life to rescue me?"

"You're not rescued yet. Let's go."

They stepped into the hall and Tristan saw Kai. A huge grin enveloped his face. "Kai!" He rushed to hug him.

"Good to see you, kid." Kai looked up at Varian. "You can handle it from here?"

Varian nodded. "Good luck, Kai."

Tristan glanced at Varian and then at Kai. "What does he mean, good luck?"

"There's something I have to do. Go with Varian and do everything he tells you. It'll keep you safe and make his ego feel better." Kai smiled at Varian. "Good luck to you, too." He turned and headed in the direction of Proctor's office.

"Come with me," Varian said. "The horses are tied to a tree outside the dome." They ran down the hall.

"What about the guards?" Tristan asked.

"We're unlikely to run into any. They're all heading to attack the bunker. If we ride quickly, we can take a more direct path the vehicles can't and get there in time to warn the others."

They came to the dome entrance. Varian pointed. "There. Can you see the horses?"

"Yes."

"We'll make a run for them. Mount a horse and follow me."

"Got it."

The boys ran to the tree and untied the horses. Seconds later, they were galloping away.

Maga gulped as she saw the domed city ahead. Even if the patrols were still on the lookout for her, there appeared to be none in sight. Nonetheless, she felt a wave of terror gazing at the city and realizing, patrols or no patrols, Dr. Carstairs would still be there waiting to make good on her threat. Maga swallowed and took a deep breath. This wasn't about her safety; it was about Donjay's. She tied her horse to a nearby tree and proceeded on foot into the city.

Once inside the familiar mansion, Maga took a cloak from a closet and covered her head with the hood. Furtively, she made her way through the mansion until she reached Donjay's room. She pushed the door open and found him lying on the bed. He blinked his eyes. "Maga? Is it really you?" He closed his eyes and shook his head. "The drug must be making me hallucinate."

Maga sat by his bedside. "Donjay, it's me. Wake up." She shook him.

"Maga? You're really here?" He tried to sit up.

"What have they done to you?"

"I'm groggy. Dr. Carstairs drugged me."

"We've got to get out of here. The bunker kids are going to attack Utopia."

Donjay shook his head. "No, no. It's the other way around: Proctor's launching an assault on the bunker."

"It's not safe in Utopia. We have to leave."

"Help me stand." Maga assisted her brother to his feet. "Wait here. I'll see Proctor and demand he guarantee your safety."

"You can't make demands of Proctor," Maga said. "Come with me. We must flee the city."

"Walk me around the room until my head clears. Then, I'll talk to Proctor." With Maga's help, Donjay staggered across the room.

"They're coming!" Fiona shouted from atop the watchtower. She clambered down and ran to the others. "At least a half-dozen vehicles identical to Kai's not-a-sports-car are headed this way. They have rifles mounted on them."

"The not-a-sports-car can hold four people," Blaine said. "That's up to twenty-four armed Utopians invading the bunker."

Corona turned to Esme. "Go back into the bunker and find out if Destine and Keiana have the defense grid ready. Tell them the Utopians are attacking and we need it now."

Esme nodded and raced off.

"Blaine, gather the younger kids and secure them inside the bunker," Covid said. "Fiona, take Nessa and Coralie inside. Then seal the door and don't let anyone open it."

Fiona brushed away a tear and nodded. Corona, Dax, and Ian huddled around Covid. "If Destine and Keiana can't get the defense grid operational, then the four of us are the bunker's last line of defense." He turned to Corona. "There's still time for you to join the others inside."

Corona shook her head. "This is all my fault. If I hadn't been so eager to explore the outside world, then the Utopians wouldn't even know we existed."

"It's not your fault," Dax said. "We have as much right to the planet as they do. Proctor's just another bully... and he'll

Chapter Twenty-Three

meet the same fate they all do." She picked up a sack of grenades. "Better grab your rifles; I hear their engines."

Covid, Corona, and Ian took their rifles and scattered as the Humvees rolled into view.

Kai peeked inside each door he passed hoping to spot Archer and Robin. He kept his bow ready in his hand, well aware he was deep in enemy territory. He opened the next door and realized it was Dr. Carstairs laboratory. He saw her bent over a Bunsen burner heating a flask. Kai started to close the door but Dr. Carstairs glanced up and saw him.

"Kai!" she exclaimed. "How delightful to see you again. Does Proctor know you're here?" She took a step toward him.

Kai raised his bow and notched an arrow. "Keep back. Where's Proctor?"

"In his study, I'd presume. I was going to begin the sperm extraction procedure with your friend Tristan but you're a much more mature specimen. Come with me to the Dairy and we'll get you strapped in."

Kai shot his arrow at her Bunsen burner, knocking it over. The fire spread to the chemical-stained tablecloth which burst into flames. "Not this time, Doctor. Besides, I think you have a fire to put out." Kai shut the door behind him and dashed down the hall, trying to recall the location of Proctor's office.

Proctor never heard them enter. Granny had trained them well in the art of stealth. The furtive siblings stood inside Proctor's study to the left and right of the door. Robin reached into her pocket and pulled out the St. Sebastian medal. Proctor looked up upon hearing it jangle in her hand.

"How did you get in here? Guards!" He realized as he was shouting, he had sent most of his men to the bunker and the remainder were on foot patrol within the city. He stared at the pair of teens, studying their attire and weapons. "Are you bunker children?"

"We're Raiders," Archer said.

Robin tossed the St. Sebastian medal onto his desk. "Is that yours?"

"My St. Sebastian medal! I thought it lost forever. Tell me, whom do I have to thank for its recovery?" Proctor's hand edged surreptitiously closer to his desk drawer as he spoke.

"I'm Archer."

"Robin, his sister."

"Such fitting names. All you need to complete the motif is some forest green outfits." His fingers wrapped around the drawer handle and slowly pulled it open. "Wherever did you find my medal?"

Robin and Archer raised their bows, aiming their arrows at Proctor. "It was at the Outpost," Archer said.

"On the ground," Robin added. "Beside my grandmother's body. We reckon Granny tore it off the neck of the man who killed her."

Proctor's eyes narrowed as his fingers wrapped around the revolver in his drawer. "Your grandmother! Yes, I see the resemblance now. You have your mother's eyes, Robin."

Robin wavered, lowering her bow by an inch. "You knew my mother?"

"He's lying, Robin."

Chapter Twenty-Three

"Now Archer takes after your father: rude, arrogant, self-righteous… I don't know what my sister saw in him." He furtively slipped the revolver from the drawer.

Archer gasped. "You're our mother's brother?"

"If you are who you say — and I've no reason to doubt your veracity, given your emotional response to my mother's death — then you may call me Uncle Proctor." He raised the revolver.

Robin and Archer drew a bead on him. "You can't shoot two targets," Archer said. "The other one will get you."

"This needn't be an awkward family reunion," Proctor said. "It's the rare individual who's capable of killing their own flesh and blood. Put down your weapons and join me in Utopia. Our family blood runs through your veins, Archer. You could be my heir apparent."

Archer shook his head. "You killed Granny, didn't you? You murdered your own mother!"

Proctor slowly panned his arm, aiming his gun at Archer.

Robin released her arrow a second before Archer shot his. Her arrow struck Proctor's hand, causing him to drop the revolver; Archer's arrow sliced into Proctor's shoulder.

"Ain't so rare after all," Robin said. "'Leastways, it must run in the family." Both teens reached into their quivers with lightning-fast reflexes and notched a second arrow, which they fired instantaneously. They continued as human perpetual motion machines until Proctor resembled a cross between a pin cushion and a porcupine.

Kai burst into the study. "I've been looking all over for you two."

"Told you this was something we had to do ourselves," Archer said.

"Yeah, I'm real bad at doing what people tell me."

241

Robin glanced at Proctor, as he tumbled from his chair and crawled toward them reaching out for help. "We done what we came fer. You want to ride back with us, Kai?"

"What about Proctor?" Kai asked.

"With that many holes in him, he's gonna bleed to death, slow and painful," Archer said. "We can stay and watch if'n you want."

"If you're ready to leave, we need to get back to the bunker," Kai said. "Proctor sent his men to attack it and they're going to need all the help they can get defending it."

"Then, let's go," Archer said. "You can ride back with me on my horse." They ran out the door past Donjay as he staggered into the study.

Dax scrambled in front of one of the oncoming Humvees, avoiding shots fired by its gunner. She pulled the pin and tossed the grenade into the turret before leaping out of the way of the blast. She reached into her sack to discover she had used her last grenade.

"It's no good," Corona said. "Dax blew up most of the vehicles but not before they discharged their passengers. They're swarming all over and our rifles are running out of bullets."

"We have to stop as many of them as we can to give Destine and Keiana enough time to get the defense grid working," Covid said. "Even if they get past us, there's six inches of titanium between them and everyone in the bunker."

"I've got some bullets left," Ian said. "I'll stand at the door and shoot anyone who tries to get in."

Covid shook his head. "No good. Their rifles could strike you from hundreds of yards away."

Chapter Twenty-Three

Corona's forlorn expression conveyed her despair. "Then... it's over."

The Utopians realized that as well from the lull in the gunfire and rose from their sheltered positions to advance on the unarmed teens.

Chapter Twenty-Four

THE UTOPIANS CHARGING FORWARD DIDN'T notice it at first. Their eyes were on the prize: the bunker and the four helpless teenagers outside no longer able to defend it. The land surrounding the besieged bunker that they had turned into a battlefield was imperceptibly morphing into a garden, but not merely any run-of-the-mill garden: a warrior's garden. Metal sprouts burst through the soil, rising a foot before bending at a 20° angle and then shooting up several more feet. The scattered black pipes began firing a steady stream of bullets in a crossfire that cut down at least half the men in seconds. The Utopians retreated, but as they did, landmines laying inert since they were planted long ago suddenly sprang to life, exploding whenever they could inflict the most casualties, as if they had a mind of their own.

Inside the bunker, in the computer terminal room, Destine and Keiana high-fived each other. "Defense grid activated and automatic lockdown engaged," Destine said. "No one's getting inside the bunker."

"Unfortunately, that includes our friends but hopefully they have the sense to keep their heads down," Keiana said. "We'll prevail today but there's nothing to prevent the Utopians from coming back."

"Or is there? What if we bring the fight to them?"

"How do you suggest we do that? This is a *defensive* grid."

"With limited offensive capabilities, according to the diary." Destine pointed to Utopia on the map on one of the computer screens. "We could use the pop-up missile launchers to fire on Utopia."

Keiana shook her head. "I thought of that. I've already done the calculations. Our missile range is limited: We could only reach the edge of the dome. We wouldn't be able to inflict citywide damage."

A sly smile crept across Destine's face. "What if we simply bombarded the edge of the dome with missile after missile?"

"It would cause significant damage in that one area but the shells wouldn't land any farther. They'd keep hitting the dome until it cracked and pieces fell over that area…"

"Have you ever seen anything with a crack where the crack didn't spread? Especially if it's constantly being pounded?"

Keiana's eyes widened. "Once the dome starts to crack, if we keep hitting it with missiles, then the cracks will run through the entire dome."

"Pieces of the dome will break off and plunge down all over the city. It'll look as if the sky is falling."

"Like the bombing of Dresden in World War II we read about in History class. The Utopians will never want to mess with us again!" Keiana's finger hovered over the missile launch button. "Is now the time for trial and error?"

Proctor reached out to Donjay as the young man entered the study. "Help me. Get Dr. Carstairs."

Donjay staggered forward, still groggy from the sedative Dr. Carstairs had given him. He stumbled several times, as the room itself was shaking from pieces of the dome — shattered by the missile barrage — repeatedly struck the building. "I was outside in the hall. I overheard you."

"Donjay, get the doctor. Please, son."

"Son? Am I your son once again? Your heir apparent? Or have you been lying to me all these years, as you lied about Maga?"

"Doctor. I need the doctor or I'll die." Different-sized chunks of the dome bounced off the roof above them, like oversized raindrops on a tin roof.

"I heard you offer to make that boy your heir— a Raider, no less! Maga was right: you're a liar and I can't wait for you to die of old age for my turn to replace you." His eyes darted about the study and fell on the poker leaning against the fireplace. Donjay reached for it and struck Proctor again and again, beating him to death. He tossed the poker aside. "The waiting's over. Utopia is mine!"

Donjay looked up at the pitter-patter of pebbles and debris striking the roof and saw Maga entering the study. "I told you to wait for me in my room. No matter. I'm glad you're here. You can help me celebrate what's destined to be the happiest day of my life."

"What are you talking about? Where's Proctor?"

Donjay glanced up at a rumbling coming from the ceiling. He saw a large crack running across it. "Maga, get out!" he shouted. Donjay staggered toward her to push Maga from the room but was too groggy to run. A loud thud reverberated through the room as a large chunk of the dome smashed through the ceiling like a meteorite. Donjay watched helplessly, horrified as the roof caved in on his sister. He stumbled toward the rubble, tossing each piece of debris aside until he saw the crushed and bloody remains lying beneath it.

"No!" he screamed. "Maga. Why, why?" He gritted his teeth and inhaled deeply and defiantly.

Dr. Carstairs burst in. "Proctor, are you all right?"

Donjay pointed to the arrow-filled corpse. "Proctor's dead. I'm in charge of Utopia now."

Dr. Carstairs gulped, absorbing the news of Proctor's demise. "We're under attack! The dome has collapsed. The sky is literally falling throughout the city."

"Attacked by whom?"

"The bunker children. Only a handful of our patrols have returned and they bring stories of carnage. Half our fleet of Humvees had to be abandoned or were destroyed; the other half sits here with no batteries to run them. And now, when we need him most, Proctor is dead."

Donjay gazed down at Maga's remains. "Not just Proctor." He looked up at Dr. Carstairs, steely-eyed. "We don't need Proctor. I shall rebuild the dome and the city. Utopia will rise again… and when it does, those responsible for this will pay with their lives."

The stars seemed particularly bright on this night. What had been a battlefield that afternoon had become a campground after dusk. A half-dozen campfires illuminated the young faces surrounding them. Archer opened a bag of marshmallows Kai had brought back from their store. They were a bit stale but he didn't mind. He stuck three on an arrow and held them over the fire. The flame would soften them. And they'd be safe to eat — as Kai had taught him, fire was the great cleanser. So their code said.

Archer offered one to his sister. Robin declined, instead snuggling up to Covid. "I'm glad I didn't shoot you that first day at the store."

Covid grinned. "Me too."

"I was right then, too — you ain't too hard on the eyes."

"And you've learned how to spell my name."

Corona saw the distant look in her brother's eyes that belied his banter. "What's troubling you, Covid?"

"Maga never came back from Utopia. I knew she'd be risking her life returning to save her brother, yet somehow I thought she'd survive. Proctor must have killed her, too."

"Proctor ain't killing no one else," Robin said. "He's worm food now... with the holes already made for the worms to burrow through."

Corbin gestured for Archer to join him. "Be right back, folks." He approached Corbin.

"Archer, I think it's time we got to know each other better," Corbin said. "I thought we might chat about your store and its merchandise. I have an exciting business proposition for you..."

A few yards away, at another campfire, Blaine and Esme were necking. Destine frowned disapprovingly. "There must be something in the air. It seems everyone is pairing off."

"Not everyone," Keiana said. "We're still single. I read in a book once that boys don't like smart girls." She tilted her head toward Dax and Coralie, who were embracing at another campfire. "Of course, not everyone needs boys."

"There's lots of options beyond the bunker," Destine said. "Robin said I could come with her and Archer the next time they visit a Raider outpost. She said some of them have a few boys our age."

Several yards away, Coralie looked up into Dax's eyes. "We're going to be safe now, right?"

Dax cradled her head. "It's an awful big world outside the bunker, and I've a hunch it's a dangerous one, too. But I'll keep you safe."

Coralie smiled. "Just like you did that day with Arlo and Nico in the classroom." She frowned and her eyes darted about the horizon. "You don't think they're out there watching us now, do you?"

Dax shook her head gently. "No, they're gone and they won't be back. Like I said, I'll keep you safe." She kissed Coralie's forehead and drew her into her bosom.

Ian approached Destine and Keiana holding a half-empty bag of marshmallows. "I saw you two sitting alone by your fire and thought you might like some of Archer's fluffy stuff."

"Marshmallows," Destine said.

"Um, yeah, that's what he called them."

"Thanks," Keiana said. "Why don't you sit down and join us?"

Ian hesitated. "Well, I'm not really a good talker. I don't read a lot of books like you two do. I spend most of my time working out."

Keiana reached out and felt his muscular arm. "I can tell." She placed a marshmallow on a stick, then paused before adding a second one. "I wonder which end goes on first?"

Ian frowned. "They look the same to me."

"So do magnets," Keiana said. "But each has a north end and a south end. If these two marshmallows were magnets and I put both same ends together, they'd repel each other." She turned the marshmallow around. "But if I put the south end up against the north end, they'd stick together like two melted marshmallows." She toasted the stick before handing it to Destine. "It's a scientific principle: opposites attract. Excuse me, I see someone I need to speak to." She left the two of them by the campfire.

She is one manipulative bitch, Destine thought. *Still...* "May I feel your muscle?" Destine asked.

"Sure," Ian said, eagerly rolling up his sleeve.

At another campfire, Tristan had his arm around Nessa as they roasted marshmallows. "I was really scared when they told me the Utopians had kidnapped you."

"I was scared, too." Tristan laughed and she found his laughter infectious. "Things could have turned really bad if Varian hadn't rescued me when he did."

"Fiona's always saying nice things about Varian. I know you don't like him but—"

Tristan shook his head. "Varian's a good guy. I shouldn't have blamed him for Lucian's death. He's just like us: a kid who makes mistakes. I guess I thought because he was older, he wasn't allowed to make mistakes. But he walked into Utopia, faced down my guard, freed me, and got me home in one piece. I don't know if I could be that brave. I saw a side of him I'd never seen before. Maybe I hadn't wanted to see it, or maybe I hadn't been looking for it. But I think it's the side Fiona sees too."

"She really likes him. He's been spending a lot of time with her lately. I may have to find a new best friend."

The QuaranTeens

"Hey, I thought we were best friends?"

Nessa shook her head. "Nah. If Fiona has a boyfriend now, I think I should have one too. I mean, I'm thirteen and I've never been kissed."

Tristan bit his lip. "Well, I'm fourteen and I've never... I mean, not exactly..." He looked around to see if anyone was watching. "You want to try it?"

"Now?"

"Keep your voice down. If I'm going to be your boyfriend, we'll have to do it sometime. Now's as good a time as any."

"All right." Nessa puckered her lips.

Tristan leaned in and kissed her quickly on the lips. "How was that?"

She moved her lips back and forth. "Try it again."

Tristan leaned in and gave her a slightly longer kiss.

Nessa smirked. "Keep trying."

Fiona and Varian stepped through the bunker's hatch. "I still think this is a bad idea," Varian said.

"Everyone's outside celebrating our victory," Fiona said. "You deserve this celebration as much as anyone."

"My presence will just make everyone feel uncomfortable. You don't have to pretend, Fiona. I know what they will think of me."

Keiana approached them. "Have you told him?"

"Not yet," Fiona said.

"Told him what?" Varian asked.

"A group of us met earlier today. We decided to form a governing council instead of having any single individual lead us."

Varian looked down at the ground. "I suppose my disastrous term as leader is responsible for that. For what it's worth, it sounds like a good idea."

252

Chapter Twenty-Four

"The council's membership will likely change over time but the initial five members were agreed on."

"If you're this happy, you must have been selected."

Keiana grinned. "They wanted someone with brains but it was close until Destine took herself out of the running. She probably figures she'll get her say so long as Covid's on the council. We also picked Dax. She has incredible inner strength and you should have seen her fighting the Utopians today."

Varian nodded. "So, the brain, the hero, the tough girl... who else to round out your council?"

Keiana pointed to Fiona. Varian smiled. "Ah, the voice of compassion to temper all the other voices. I approve." He kissed Fiona. "A wise choice, Keiana. I'm sure your little group will steer us through the tough times ahead." Varian turned to Fiona. "I suppose we should celebrate your new position. Which campfire would you like to sit at?"

"Wait," Keiana said. "You're forgetting the fifth member."

"Who else? Kai?"

Keiana shook her head, laughing. "You don't choose a rule-breaker to be a rule-maker. We chose you, Varian."

Varian shook his head in disbelief. "No, the other's won't—"

"It was unanimous," Fiona said.

Varian shook his head. "What do I bring to the council? Failure? Poor judgment?"

"Leadership," Keiana said. "Oh, not by yourself. But Corbin told us what you said when you went off to rescue Tristan: 'I'm not *the* leader but I am *a* leader.' You can be one of our leaders, Varian."

"Tristan." He shook his head, remembering how he'd told Fiona he couldn't bear to see the look in Tristan's eyes whenever they passed in the halls. "No, I don't think..."

"It was Tristan's idea," Fiona said. "He nominated you for the council."

"Tristan did?" Varian looked up in surprise. "It wasn't one of his jokes, was it?"

"We're meeting in the morning after breakfast," Keiana said. "Don't be late."

Several yards away, the campfire embers were fading. Kai wrapped his arms around Corona as they gazed at the stars. "Space is really big," Kai said.

"So is the Earth," Corona said.

"You know, each of those vehicles left behind by the Utopians had two batteries. If they were all charged and stored in the back of the not-a-sports-car, we could drive an incredible distance swapping them out before we'd need to find a recharging generator."

Corona smiled at him. "I was hoping you'd say that. Of course, the new council might make rules against going off exploring."

Kai gave her a puzzled look. "What are rules?"